Some Prefer Stilettos

A Trunk Doctor Mystery

Sara McFerrin

2020

To SueAnn —
Thanks for reading and advising, I think we ended up with something good.

Sara

ISBN 10: 0-9994785-5-4
ISBN 13: 978-0-9994785-5-4

Cover Design: Rose Mermoud

Contact the author at: www.saramcferrin.com or saramcferrin@mediacombb.net

In Memory of
Cynthia Watson
Gone too soon - Never forgotten

Acknowledgements

A special thanks to many for their support and vital contributions on completing this book. Darlene Watkins, Sue Ann Beer, and Regina Fouts read the second draft and helped me see things from the reader's point of view. Sue Cronkite was most helpful as a developmental editor. Thank you, Sue, for helping when you were busy marketing your own book, "Louette's Wake." And special thanks go to Jerri Cachero and Rossana Tarantini for reading and reviewing the first draft.

I consulted Pete Howard on heavy equipment and how it functions. Kim Plyler Kerrinnes' input on drug addiction added an insight readers will appreciate. And of course, my granddaughter Charlotte Rose Mermoud has designed and illustrated a fabulous cover. A special thanks to our unsung hero; my daughter Geni. In addition to putting up with me, she invests time and expertise in "our" books. The photo on the cover of "Some Prefer Stilettos" belongs to Geni Mermoud. She also formats and does all computer-related things.

My goal is to write clean, clever, engaging mysteries, and to create book friends for avid readers.

I hope you enjoy sleuthing with Jix and Abby Gayle.

Sara McFerrin

Books by Sara McFerrin

Curiosity Club Mystery Series:

Southern Ladies' Curiosity Club
Whatever Happened to Mildred?
Sunken Secrets
The Ghost of Stupid Mistakes

Southern Quickies:

Conversations: Beebe's Facelift
Conversations: Marian's Last Wish
Conversations: In Good Hands

Trunk Doctor Mystery Series:

What She Saw

Other Titles:

Whistlin' Stardust

Raney Days: David G. Raney Family
& Their Antebellum Home

Chapter One

For the third time Eva Helton read carefully composed words written on crisp, fine linen stationery bearing the letterhead of the prestigious law firm of Cyrix, Satterfield, and Levinstein.

According to the letter, the property was to be vacated within sixty days. Stunned, she was left with no choice but to call a meeting of the tenants as soon as possible. Her afternoon plans could not be rescheduled, thus the gathering would have to wait until the following morning. It would take that long to summon enough courage to deliver what, undoubtedly, would be distressing news to tenants and their families, but better they hear it from her than some other way.

Not being an early morning person, interacting with others in a pleasant manner at eight o'clock was seldom Eva's first choice of how to begin a day. Nevertheless, she was anxious to be relieved of the grim burden, so the earlier the better.

She removed her reading glasses attached to a gold chain and dropped them to dangle around her neck. It occurred to her the tenants might have also received notification. If so, she needed to leave the premises or face an onslaught of phone calls.

Eva reasoned that as building superintendent, she would be among the first to know if changes were forthcoming. Two weeks ago, three men dressed in expensive, tailored suits with shiny silk ties knotted like decorative Adam's apples had toured the building with Arnold Webber, a local banker often seen in the newspaper or on local television at ribbon cutting ceremonies. Eva was puzzled that common social etiquette had not compelled them to inform the in-house manager of their intentions. Had she not heard the men talking in the hallway as they exited the building, she would have never known they'd set foot on the property.

Grasping the letter with both hands, she inhaled deeply and exhaled with an audible sigh. Eva fully expected old Mr. Devlin on the eighth floor to rant and rave even more than he had when the couple in the apartment above him had taken up Flamenco dancing. There was no need to guess as to Mrs. Lockhart's response...the woman cried when mail delivery was delayed. Belinda Watson—always strapped for cash even though she worked two jobs—and her four kids had moved into the building a few months ago. Lord only knew what would become of them. And Ebony Anderton and her handicapped son Troy's destinies were as unpredictable as a good hair day.

She had rather babysit ten two-year-olds for two days than to be the bearer of ill tidings. Her position at Fairmont Manor had landed the unpleasant task in her lap.

Placing the devastating notice on her desk, Eva pulled the tenant roster from the drawer. She glanced at her wristwatch and decided she had time before her first appointment to make one call. There was no question as to which tenant she should contact first.

Marigold Fairmont occupied the entire tenth floor. Her parents, Joel and Catherine Fairmont, had completed construction of Fairmont Manor in 1906, four years prior to Marigold's debut. Seventy-nine years later, the Fairmont's only child slept in the room overlooking the park across the street, the same room in which she'd been born.

Eva started to dial Marigold's number, changed her mind, and replaced the receiver in its cradle. This was too important for a phone call; if she hurried, and if she didn't stay long, she had time to go upstairs and talk with Lady Fairmont—a courtesy title of no legal significance that was used mostly to reference Marigold Fairmont when not in her presence.

Good manners dictated she should call first. Based on past phone exchanges, Eva knew her intended brief conversation would be anything but, since the short, roly-poly woman with hair dyed flaming-red gave new meaning to loquaciousness.

On second thought, no need to call. It was Wednesday, and every Wednesday the star socialite of Fairmont Manor hosted bridge club at three in the afternoon. She would be expecting company and was sure to be at home barking orders at her maid Rossana. Eva had an excuse to cut the visit short and be on her way as Marigold was preparing for guests, and she, Eva, had a busy day planned.

The elevator climbed at a snail's pace from the first to the tenth floor. Expecting to be greeted by a midmorning flurry of activity as Rossana rushed about and Sonya, the cook, prepared tantalizing tidbits for a dozen bridge players, Eva was instead surprised by an eerie stillness.

She stepped onto polished French Vanilla marble floors bordered by Belgium Black, Alicante White, and Rouge Griotte marble, artfully woven into a linear design around the perimeter of the room.

The door softly shuffled and then closed behind her with a muted clunk.

"Rossana," she called. No one answered.

Three doors led from the foyer into the expansive apartment. Two black lacquered, Art Deco-style doors were closed. The main entrance, a brass door with a striking sunburst motif, stood ajar.

"Marigold," Eva shouted. "Hello! Sonya! Yoohoo, anyone?"

The hair on the nape of her neck stood on end. A sinking feeling that something bad had happened led to fleeting consideration to call on her first-floor neighbor Cathy Kessler to help investigate.

Unlikely, but possible, the bridge club may have been cancelled or the gathering had been moved to another location, for reasons she could not imagine.

"Plleaseeee." A barely audible plea sounded from inside the living quarters.

Eva rushed to the partially opened door and slowly pushed it. The elegant room furnished in Art Deco was in total disarray!

Filled with trepidation, her eyes swept the chaotic scene of overturned club chairs and game tables, books no longer neatly stacked on a mirrored console table, sharp-edged shards from a broken Lalique vase, an upended antique Japanese side table. Three decks of playing cards were scattered on the parquet floor like rainbow sprinkles.

"Marigold! Rossana!" Eva shouted frantically.

"Help. Please, help me."

Eva's heart pounded like a jungle drum as she followed Marigold's live-in cook's faint cry.

"Oh, dear God," she grimaced at a battered and bleeding sight.

"Sonya! What happened? Where is Miss Fairmont?"

She fumbled to untie Sonya's apron, wadded it, and applied pressure to a head wound. Helping the injured woman to a sitting position, Eva propped her against the wall and placed a Turkish, velvet throw pillow within reach behind Sonya's head.

Eva repeated, "Where is Miss Fairmont? Where is Rossana?"

Sonya paled. Her eyes rolled back in her head just before she slipped into unconsciousness and collapsed in a heap.

Eva Helton ran from room to room calling for Marigold

Fairmont or Rossana but found neither. Quickly, she located a phone.

"9-1-1. Send an ambulance and the police!" Struggling to focus, she gave a summary of the situation and the address. Rushing back to Sonya, Eva checked the still unconscious woman's pulse while she chanted that help was on the way and everything would be all right, even though there were no assurances such would be the case.

Helpless to do anything more, Eva headed downstairs to wait outside for the ambulance. She hoped to expedite matters by leading the paramedics to Sonya.

Eva's nerves were stretched as tight as a rubber band. She leaned against the elevator wall and tried to force her thoughts into some semblance of order. Marigold's only living relative came to mind.

Detouring by way of her apartment, Eva rummaged through the middle desk drawer for her address book. Fingering the F tab, she fumbled for her suspended glasses, fit them on her face after several attempts, and felt the chains brush against her cheeks. Her index finger traced down the page landing on Margee Fairmont's name and number.

Unrelated to Marigold by blood (Margee Jixson had married Marigold's first cousin, David Fairmont now deceased), Margee and her family visited frequently and always included Marigold in their family holiday celebrations.

The ring tone monotonously buzzed. Eva nervously drummed her fingertips on the receiver. She stretched the coiled phone cord to the window facing the street and parted the blinds with her thumb and forefinger to watch for the ambulance.

Eva would ask Margee to come as soon as possible, and to bring her daughter Jix Haynes. It was common knowledge that Jix had a knack for making sense out of mysterious circumstances.

Chapter Two

"Careful. Don't scuff it," Jix Haynes, aka the Trunk Doctor, cautioned.

Earl Jones grunted. The Trunk Doctor's only employee had manhandled old trunks like a rodeo wrangler for six years and had never scuffed a fresh paint job. "Jack done a good job spraying it," he said.

"I'll say." The finished product pleasantly surprised Jix. "Jack Blain is a wizard with a paint sprayer. When he sold his paint store and retired, I was relieved to hear he planned to do small jobs in his workshop. Neither he nor I could envision a wardrobe steamer trunk painted navy blue." They stood back and admired the chest-high trunk. Jix unsnapped the clasps and swung the hinged halves open.

"Old trunks have soul. They cast enchanted spells," she said.

Earl understood and agreed.

"What you got planned for the inside?" he asked.

"The client wants everything inside and out navy blue. It's her favorite color."

He frowned. "Sounds boring to me. Did she want a semi-gloss finish? You usually stick to matte finishes." His opinion as to whether he liked the dark blue transformation hung in the balance.

Jix glanced at five drawers stacked on a table. The drawers filled the right-hand side like a chest of drawers. Hangers fit in the left-hand side of the trunk.

"Semi-gloss is not my choice. The trunk owner has a vision of the finished product. I hope I can come even close to what she envisions. You know I like old things to look old. I'm going to bring a bit of interest with texture. Being as I have no choice of color, I found a ribbed pattern of upholstery material thin enough to cover the drawer fronts. I'll line the trunk interior and inside the drawers with a satin fabric to add another texture. And I'm going to wrap the hangers in grosgrain ribbon...navy blue in color, of course. What do you think?"

"Anything you decide is okay with me," he joked. Earl loaded the cumbersome trunk on a dolly.

"Throw that old bedspread over it," Jix shouted, as he vanished through the doorway to a building covered in vinyl siding. "I'll be in the office if you need me."

The two-room outbuilding was the last stop for trunks. Natural light streamed in, and the rooms were free from outside dust and dirt making it the perfect place for Jix to custom design each trunk.

More than thirty antique trunks, previously exiled to storage sheds, barns, or damp basements and left to be tortured by time, had been rescued and destined for a miracle makeover.

Jix was designer and decorator. Her husband Bill's day job with Mid-State Mortgage left him to play trunk surgeon nights and weekends. He built trays, replaced missing parts, and handled any task that required a hammer or saw.

A repurposed laundry room just off the kitchen had been

converted into an office that doubled as a pocket of privacy when Jix needed a moment to gather her thoughts. The pretty, natural blonde in her fifties poured a cup of coffee and doctored it with milk and sugar. Lost in thought, she swirled a spoon in the brew as she eased into her desk chair.

Overhead, a fluorescent bulb flickered.

Was it flickering more this day than yesterday or was it her imagination? She moved papers around until she located a self-stick pad. Prepared to write a note asking Earl to replace the bulb before he left for the day, she was surprised to find a note she'd written several days before. Ripping the page from the pad, she stuck it on her shirt as a reminder to jog Earl's memory.

"Jix! Knock, knock." Margee Fairmont opened the door and rushed in with Dinah, a chubby, adorable toddler astride her hip. "Jix, Eva Helton just called. Something is terribly wrong."

"What's happened?" she asked, reaching for her granddaughter.

Daughter Carol and little Dinah had chosen not to join Carol's husband, Scotty, when he had seized an opportunity to teach English in China and Thailand. Carol was dedicated to her job as a home-care nurse, and Scotty's mission was only for eight months, so she moved back home temporarily.

Margee clasped her hands. "I'm not certain," she said. "An ambulance arrived as Eva was trying to tell me. I think she said Marigold is missing and we need to get over there as soon as possible. She specified that you come too!"

A mostly-beagle named Willowdean wandered in. Jix put Dinah down to greet her much loved, canine companion.

"Come on, Mother. Let's go to the kitchen."

She led her mother, the toddler, and the dog to the table and pulled out a chair. "Now sit down and start over. Tell me exactly what Eva said…word for word."

Margee willed her racing heart to slow down. Jix gathered Dinah in her arms, and they sat down at the table.

Margee Fairmont repeated her disturbing conversation with Eva. She then added, "If Marigold is missing, then we can assume the ambulance wasn't for her. We need to be on our way, but it is almost time for Dinah's lunch and nap."

"We don't know the extent of the situation, so Dinah doesn't need to go with us." She kissed Dinah's curly head and put her down to play. "I'll go; you stay here until Carol comes—this is her short day. She'll be home in a couple of hours. Oh! Abby Gayle is on her way—we were going to an estate sale. When she arrives, tell her to come to Fairmont Manor."

She leaned to kiss her mother on the forehead and blew kisses to Dinah and Willowdean as she headed out the door.

"Tell Earl I'm gone." She grabbed her keys off a hook by the door and hurried outside.

Jix Haynes did not hesitate to accommodate Eva even though her availability wasn't due to time on her hands. She ran a business, kept a husband happy, looked after her Mother who'd come to live with Jix and Bill when Jix's dad, David Fairmont, had passed away, and she also helped with her granddaughter.

As Jix climbed into her truck with signs on the doors advertising the Trunk Doctor, Abby Gayle Kamp turned into the driveway. Jix backed the truck beside her soul sister and best friend's car and lowered the passenger window.

"Perfect timing!" she called to blue-eyed, raven-haired Abby Gayle. "Something has come up; get in. I'll fill you in on the way."

Abby Gayle opened the door and hopped in.

"What's up?" she asked, slinging her pocketbook to rest on the seat between them.

Jix told of Eva's phone call.

"Missing!" Abby Gayle exclaimed. "With all due respect, if someone has taken Marigold as hostage, they'll return her in the best interest of their sanity. She'll talk them into a tizzy."

"Abby Gayle Kamp! Shame on you! I love Marigold."

10

"I love her too, but you know it's true. And why are you wearing a sticky note?"

Chapter Three

"Oh my!" Jix exclaimed as they approached the architecturally prestigious, brick tower.

Curious watchers had gathered from the park across the street. Uniformed officers directed both people and vehicular traffic.

"There's no place to park." Abby Gayle scanned the area for a vacant spot.

Jix turned down a side street. "Let's try the parking lot in back or in the alley."

Once they'd pulled beside the last car at the end of a packed row, and declared it to be a parking space—the truck was clearly outside the yellow lines—they went around the building to the front entrance. An officer at the door stopped them. Margee had called to say Jix was on the way. Eva expected they would be turned away and went out to explain the women had come at her request.

No sooner had the ladies stepped inside than Juliet Pratt, a long-time resident on a fact-finding mission, exited the elevator. Eva invited Jix and Abby Gayle to go inside her apartment and make themselves at home.

News that something out of the ordinary had occurred had reached the tenants and neighbors by way of a wailing ambulance siren. Eva reassured inquiring persons that everything was under control for the moment. She also informed each that it was in their best interest to attend an important meeting to be held in her apartment at eight the following morning. Chances of her remembering whom she had told of the upcoming gathering and who needed to be contacted were little to none. Before bedtime, she would call each tenant to make sure no one was overlooked.

Juliet was not easily pacified. She wouldn't leave until she knew why a police officer was stationed at the front door.

The sight of Juliet Pratt sparked the realization that very soon ten women would be arriving for an afternoon of bridge. If her memory served Eva correctly, Mrs. Pratt was a member of the bridge club.

"Oh, Juliet! You are a godsend."

Juliet stepped back. Changing the subject to avoid telling what had taken place wasn't going to work. Juliet Pratt had lived too long to fall for that old trick.

Eva asked, "Are you a member of the bridge club?"

"Yes, I am. Why?"

"Dear Juliet, the other members need to be notified that the bridge club meeting has been cancelled. Something has come up, and Marigold won't be able to host today. Will you contact the women and tell them of the change in plans?"

"Where's Marigold? She always hosts the club on Wednesdays."

"She and Rossana were suddenly called away. I don't know all the details, just that they left unexpectedly, and I need your help to save the ladies a trip. This is very important, Juliet. Marigold would never have deliberately chosen to leave this to us, but unforeseen circumstances changed her plans, and we must not let her down. May I count on you to contact the other members immediately, so they don't get dressed and come here for nothing?"

Juliet clamped her lips tight and raised an eyebrow while she mulled over the situation. "You aren't going to tell me where she is, are you?"

"I don't know where she is. I just know that something unexpected has occurred, and we need to cancel this afternoon's meeting. I'll fill you in on details as they are revealed to me. Can I count on your help?"

Juliet recognized the earmarks of a serious situation. She knew she could be part of the problem or part of the solution. Wisely, she chose. "Fine. I'll contact the others. Got any idea why there is a police officer at the elevator door that opens into Marigold's foyer?"

Eva rubbed her forehead and ran her fingers through her hair. "Thank you, Juliet for contacting the ladies. Thank you. Trust me on this, please. Come to my apartment at eight in the morning. I have news to discuss with everyone, and I may have news from Marigold also. Just trust me, Juliet. Please."

The well-coiffed woman with fine wrinkles above her upper lip looked into Eva's pleading eyes. "I'll see that everyone is notified, and Dan and I will be at the meeting in the morning… if I can get the old goat out of bed that early. Expect him to be ill as a hornet, but he'll want to come," she said of her husband. Juliet turned to leave and then spun around to ask, "Shall I bring a coffee cake?"

"That would be wonderful." A surge of both relief and gratitude washed over Eva. "I so appreciate your help, and Juliet, I promise, soon as I have news of Marigold, you will be the first I'll call."

The door slid shut, and a slight shimmy-shudder launched the elevator for the fifth floor. Eva rejoined Jix and Abby Gayle, taking the phone off the hook to silence the steady stream of calls.

Wrung out emotions from a traumatic morning began to subside, leaving a tired numbness. The widowed caretaker's shoulders slumped as she sat down on the sofa.

To rehash the morning's events, she began with the letter that had arrived by courier. She ended with how she had discovered Sonya and vandalism on the tenth floor. These incidents, she stated, of the utmost importance, paled in comparison to the urgency of finding Marigold and Rossana.

Jix said, "The police will search the building just in case Marigold and Rossana are still on the property. If they've left the premises, which route would their captors have taken?"

"I didn't hear anyone leave by the front entrance. A buzzer sounds when the door is opened, but I don't always hear it. I slept later than usual this morning due to a fitful night with a minor discomfort that comes and goes; during the night, I took medication to get to sleep, so, if anyone entered or left, I didn't hear the buzzer."

Nor would she have heard the door buzz when she was in the shower, she added. "The freight elevator is locked. I have the only key, so they didn't leave that way. To get from the tenth floor, they—and I say they, as I suppose one or more persons took Marigold and Rossana—would have had to take the elevator, the stairs, the outside fire escape, or gone on the roof and been picked up by a helicopter."

Abby Gayle stifled a grin. "You've thought this through thoroughly, haven't you?" *A helicopter?* "Let's just explore the most likely ways they would have left the building, starting with the front door."

Jix asked, "Who usually comes on a daily basis and would have been inside the building today?"

"Around six, the paper boy leaves the papers; the postman comes around ten and drops the mail in the mail chute," she pointed to the door, "I sort it and put it in the tenants' individual mail boxes. You know where the mail boxes are in the foyer." Both Jix and Abby Gayle acknowledged with a nod they knew of the wall of brass lock boxes.

Eva elaborated on the surprise arrival of a letter courier. "And a bicycle courier came around nine to deliver the letter. He was a young man in a hurry, as delivery people are. Nothing unusual about him, just a kid doing his job."

At Jix's request, Eva retrieved the letter from the desk and handed it to her.

Scanning the page, Jix was shocked and speechless. She laid the letter aside to refocus on the more important matter of the moment. "I don't know what to say about this. Neither Mother nor Marigold has mentioned any property changes, but for now, there are more important issues. We need to think about when the abduction took place...during the night, before daylight, early this morning? If Rossana and Sonya came to work, that would give us a starting point time wise, but that is, as we know, not the case."

Eva replied, "No, they live with Marigold. When the building was built in the early nineteen hundreds, providing housing for servants was common. Three rooms off the kitchen have been home to Rossana and Sonya for the ten years I've been building superintendent. I don't know when they first moved here. It is a safe assumption the Fairmonts always employed domestic help."

The women sat quietly while Jix read the letter. She then passed it to Abby Gayle.

"Well, this is shocking news, to put it mildly." Abby Gayle looked up from the page; a baffled expression masked her face. "The letter doesn't state that the property has sold. It just says the building is to be vacated."

Jix was at a loss for a reasonable explanation. "Fairmont Foundation would never sell this place as long as Marigold is alive."

Eva commented, "I don't know to what extent Marigold has a say-so in matters. The property is owned by The Foundation, as far as I know."

Jix replied, "Mother is on the Board of Trustees; she knows about Marigold's trust and how The Foundation functions. I've never had any reason to know, but I'll look into it. I simply do not believe that Marigold would willingly agree to leave or sell the property. This is her home…the only home she has ever known."

The women agreed unanimously. Jix continued, "Let's take a look at the apartment. I suppose as a crime scene, it is closed off."

"It is. There is an officer in the foyer. The forensic people may still be going over things. The first priority was to attend to Sonya." Eva resisted a flashback of the good-hearted, Danish woman—who could transform a dead chicken into a lip-smacking delicacy—lying injured and helpless. "As soon as I can get away, I'll go to the hospital."

Jix explained, "When Carol gets home, Mother can check on Sonya and let us know how she is. I'll call her."

"Oh, good! I'm anxious to know." Eva continued, "I've tried to calm the residents, but I could do with a bit of calming myself. And I've told the investigators everything I know. They've asked me not to leave as they may want to talk to me later today." Eva reflected before continuing. "I'd won a free afternoon at the new health club and spa that opened this week, but it was only for today. That ship sailed without me," she bemoaned.

Moved with compassion, Jix slid across the sofa. She put her arm around the woman admired for her gentle, commonsensical nature, as well as her commitment to the residents. Some had become like extended family to Eva.

"Who are the investigating officers? Do you remember their names?"

"One is a woman…dark hair, dark eyes, dark skin. She is

very courteous and very professional. She may still be upstairs."

Jix jumped to her feet just as Abby Gayle did the same. They slapped a high-five and yelled, "Avonelle Bird! Hallelujah!"

Startled by their abrupt response, Eva looked on with a quizzical expression. The sleuthsome twosome explained that Detective Bird was a friend...a good friend.

Jix commented, "It's not always what you know but who you know. This will make things much easier for us. As long as we don't get in the way, Detective Bird will not object to our efforts to find Marigold and Rossana."

Chapter Four

Jix pushed the "up" arrow and quipped that she sometimes imagined Jay Gatsby waiting when she stepped into Marigold's foyer.

"The Art Deco theme screams jazz age. Makes me feel like a flapper girl." She twisted her feet, kicked up her heels, and bobbed her head in sync with an imaginary string of pearls she swung round and round. Jix dancing the Charleston provided a pleasant respite from a sense of impending doom, albeit momentarily.

Abby Gayle chuckled. "Well, you lead the way Daisy Buchanan; we'll follow."

They waited for the elevator to descend to the first floor. When the door slid open, Detective Bird and her partner Joe Martino stepped out.

"Hey, you two!" A smile broke across Avonelle Bird's face. "I thought there might be a Fairmont connection with Jix."

"My dad and Marigold were first cousins. What do you think has happened? Abby Gayle and I have just arrived." As an after thought, she added, "Mother will come when Carol gets home from work."

Detective Bird turned toward a tall, Latin American man with a twinkle in his eyes, "You remember Detective Martino, don't you?"

Jix and Abby Gayle knew the amiable detective and exchanged polite greetings. Bird asked him to check on the progress of the building search and stay until the forensic crew finished. Martino stated he would meet her later at the precinct.

"If you folks have time, I'd like to ask a few questions," the lady detective said.

"Let's go to my apartment." Eva led the way back across the hall to her front door. Her empty stomach had begun to complain. She had skipped breakfast, and there had been time for only two cups of coffee—gulped rather than sipped; a most unpleasant way to experience an otherwise enjoyable part of any morning.

"It's past lunchtime. I have half a ham and cheese quiche leftover from last night." She held the door while the ladies entered the small but cozy living room.

Eva mentally inventoried refrigerator contents and reported, "And I have macaroni salad from Stockman's Deli. Please stay for lunch; we can talk things over while we eat. Shall I warm up the quiche?" She remembered another purchase the day before from the deli. "Oh, there's sliced turkey for a sandwich...and kosher pickles.

"Won't you stay?" She hoped they would say yes. Fending off a hunger headache was rapidly becoming a matter of top priority. The ladies welcomed the offer and insisted they help.

Eva's tiny kitchen had comfortable working room for no more than two slim bodies or one generously proportioned cook. Even so, the guests pitched in to set the table and pour iced tea while their hostess warmed the main entree.

Jix found a spot on limited counter space where she spread mayo on bread and assembled two turkey sandwiches and placed a half on each of four plates, leaving room for a slice of cheesy quiche. Abby Gayle stuck a serving spoon in a plastic container of macaroni salad and opened a carryout carton containing three whole kosher pickles.

A chair tucked under each end of a maple drop-leaf table pushed against the wall made two; Eva brought another chair from her dressing table and asked Abby Gayle to get the desk chair. The table converted to a small, round surface where everyone sat down to an impromptu meal.

"Bet you hadn't planned on hosting a luncheon today," Abby Gayle joked, as she unfolded a napkin and spread it in her lap.

"I hadn't planned on anything that has occurred today." From a generous portion of elbow macaroni with mayo dressing, Eva forked olives and corralled them to the side of the plate. "What do you think has happened to Marigold and Rossana?" she asked Detective Bird.

"I don't know. A thorough search of the building has produced nothing to go on. Mrs. Helton doesn't know who would have reason to harm Miss Fairmont. Do you or Abby Gayle know of anyone? And, I need you both to look over her apartment and tell me if you think anything is missing. I'd like for your mother to come as soon as she can and do the same. We need to determine if this is a robbery gone wrong."

"Mother'll be here soon. She's going by the hospital to check on Sonya. They won't give information over the phone."

"I gave the detective Sonya's niece's phone number." Eva kept emergency contact numbers on most of the residents.

Detective Bird replied, "I'll call the hospital and get an update. Please call your mother and tell her to come here instead. And I contacted the niece." In between bites of quiche, she asked, "Who are Miss Fairmont's close friends and acquaintances? I hope to talk to someone who may give us a lead."

Eva laid her fork on the plate and took a sip of tea. "Aaron Williams. He works as chauffeur, butler when the occasion calls

for one, and in a roundabout way, he serves as a bodyguard…
let's just say he's very protective of her. Aaron must be in his late
sixties and not in the best of health. I believe he has arthritis. Is
it arthritis or a bad back, Jix?"

Jix answered, "I'm not sure…maybe both. A few times Aaron
has escorted Marigold to events when Waldo wasn't available."

"Bodyguard? Waldo?" Bird queried. "Who's Waldo?"

"Rich and well known equals a need for a bodyguard. Aaron
Williams does not fit the stereotype." Jix summed up the
situation.

Abby Gayle added, "No offense intended, but not everyone
is enamored with Marigold. I wouldn't say she has enemies, but
she has crossed swords with several people over the years—some
who live in this building, some previous tenants."

Even though Abby Gayle had spoken the truth, Jix was
uncomfortable discussing Marigold's shortcomings.

Eva smiled. "It is common knowledge the Grand Lady
of Fairmont Manor can be a handful if challenged. She is a
passionate woman, that's for sure, but people who know her
also know she has a heart of gold. She has many friends."

Detective Bird finished her sandwich and chased it down
with a last swallow of tea. She put her plate in the sink and
refilled her glass, then sat back down and asked, "Who are
her close friends and frequent visitors? We are talking to every
tenant in the building to ask if anyone heard or saw anything
unusual. So far, no one has. And who is Waldo?"

"Well, as we've said, Aaron Williams, the all-around
handyman visits on a regular basis…perhaps daily. And, of
course, Waldo. I don't know him well," Eva said.

Bird cocked an eyebrow and cast a let-me-talk-to-your-
manager look in Jix's direction.

She caught the drift and responded, "Waldo has been
Marigold's gentleman friend for about three years…wouldn't
you say?" she inquired of Abby Gayle.

"Sounds right."

"What's his full name and what do you know about him?" Bird asked.

"His name is Waldo Allicott. He owns Allicott Aeronautics. Marigold calls him Wally. He doesn't live here. He has several homes in various locations."

"Back to this Aaron Williams," Bird said. "How long has he worked for Miss Fairmont?"

"At least twenty-five years," answered Jix and Abby Gayle.

The detective wondered, "What about a previous gentleman friend? Who did she see before Mr. Allicott?"

Jix and Abby Gayle filled in details about Mr. Mixon, who'd succumbed to a heart attack at age ninety-two.

Eva resumed her hosting duties with apologies for a limited choice of desserts; actually, the choice was limited to one. She asked who would like Oreos and milk. Three orders were placed.

Avonelle Bird, the tallest woman present, volunteered to reach wide, squatty, seldom-used juice glasses stored on an upper cabinet shelf. While Eva rinsed the glasses and filled them with milk, the detective called the hospital and then checked in with Martino.

Jix phoned her mother to hear that Bill had stopped by for lunch. Margee reported she'd made him a sandwich and told him of the bizarre events of the morning.

Bird made phone calls then returned to the kitchen to dunk cookies.

"I caught Mother in the nick of time; she was just leaving. She's on her way here," Jix reported.

"Good. We'll go up to the apartment for you to determine if anything is missing. I phoned Detective Martino and the search of the building is complete. There is no trace of Miss Fairmont or her maid. Unfortunately there is no change in Sonya Munhall's condition."

Chapter Five

Margee's wandering gaze came to rest on an oak and black-lacquered credenza. "Galapago is missing," she said.

"What? Who?" Bird perked up.

Jix made a circle with her index fingers and thumbs. "A white marble turtle the size of a saucer. He lives here." She patted a vacant spot on the sleek sideboard.

The detective hoped to remember to tell Martino they had bagged Galapago. "We took it. It is the weapon used in the assault."

Eva slapped her hand to her chest in an effort to keep her startled heart intact. "Oh, my goodness! No wonder the poor woman lost consciousness. If I saw the turtle at all, I must have assumed it was knocked off the credenza."

"Whoever struck her, tossed or dropped it where we found it partially under this chair." The policewoman pointed at an upholstered chair that resembled a one-armed seashell. Earlier, Avonelle Bird had commented to her partner that there wasn't a stick of ordinary furniture in sight.

Margee swallowed a sob. "This is tragic. Poor Sonya wouldn't hurt a fly." Eyeing the remains of the broken twelve thousand-dollar Lalique vase, she said, "And Marigold's beautiful things scattered and ruined." A plea for answers targeted the detective, "Where are Marigold and Rossana? We must find them! We must!"

Jix rushed to her mother. "Mom, it'll be all right. They've been missing a matter of hours, and Detective Bird is doing everything she can. We'll find them. And besides, Marigold is capable of taking care of herself. If she can't escape, she'll talk them into letting her go."

Jix disliked resorting to such impractical speculation, but she was short on reasonable possibilities.

The ladies moved around the trashed rooms, stepping over broken items and disheveled furniture. Tears stung Margee's eyes. "This is heartbreaking. How could this have happened?" She looked to the others for an explanation.

Referring to the overturned game tables, Jix surmised, "This must have taken place not long before you arrived, Eva. The card tables were set for the bridge club."

"That makes sense," Abby Gayle stated. "Rossana and Sonya set the tables up after breakfast on Wednesdays. I'd guess around nine o'clock…give or take half an hour. I know because I once helped when Sonya had strained her back and Marigold called on me."

Detective Bird noted this in a pocketsize spiral notebook.

Jix said, "You said the building has been searched, but are you aware that this old building has many places that are no longer used? Places where someone could hide or be hidden."

She had the policewoman's attention, "Such as?"

Margee answered, "Well, for one, there is an elevator that was used by domestic workers…a service elevator. Is it still operative?" she asked Eva.

"As far as I know, the elevator is operative but the entrance door at the back of the building is locked. All these old buildings have or had service elevators. Domestic help wasn't permitted to enter by the front entrance. Follow me." Eva led the way to the kitchen. She and Abby Gayle swung open a floor-to-ceiling shelving unit hinged to the wall to reveal the obsolete elevator.

Bird stepped forward and pushed the button. The door to the two-person lift played tug o' war with the latch for a few seconds before releasing. Onlookers held their breath.

The elevator was empty.

Margee elaborated, "I recall that sometime in the late nineteen sixties use of this elevator was discontinued and the doors covered on the other nine floors. Marigold wanted this one to be accessible. David told me at the time that Marigold had concealed the lift with this shelving unit. If my memory serves me, the lift was eliminated for security reasons. Tenants used it as a back door. It was decided that an outside fire escape met requirements as an emergency exit. At that time, a buzzer was installed on the front entrance and a better locking mechanism on the freight elevator."

Detective Bird said, "Well, obviously our missing couple is not in the elevator nor did they use it. Anything else I need to know about no longer used areas?"

"There are dumbwaiters in every apartment. They're still used by mostly older tenants. Others bring their groceries up in the elevator. Did you search the roof?" Abby Gayle asked. She hadn't been on the roof, but basic rationale concluded there would be some type of accessible housing for pulleys, gears, motors, and such.

"Yes, there is a shed on the roof. Neither Detective Martino nor I saw anything out of place. Officers searched the basement, the incinerator chute, the fire escape, and both the sixth and ninth floors that are vacant."

"Vacant?" Margee's eyebrows shot up to her hairline.

Eva nodded. "The building needs major repairs, especially on those two floors. Both plumbing and electrical issues are extensive and expensive to repair. To leave the units vacant is the decision of the Fairmont Foundation. I've gotten estimates as to what it will take to correct the problems. Their decision was not to rent those apartments until money has been appropriated. So far, no one has contacted me to proceed with the repairs."

"Did Marigold know things weren't being maintained?" Margee asked.

"Mr. Clifford Purefoy and his grandson Bryson are my liaisons with the Foundation. I prefer dealing with the elder Mr. Purefoy. Both men have asked me specially not to discuss anything concerning the building with Marigold."

"That's odd," said both Jix and Abby Gayle.

Chapter Six

Given the go ahead, Eva and Margee set things back in order and cleared away all that was broken or scattered. Meanwhile, Jix and Abby Gayle took the elevator to the basement to conduct a search of their own. They planned to start at the bottom of the building and work their way to the top.

Having located a panel of light switches, they pondered where to start their search. The cavernous area was dimly lit with ancient, randomly placed, mismatched fixtures or dangling, naked light bulbs. The far side of the area remained dark. Jix fumbled with the switches until she flipped one that illuminated the remaining half of the space.

"I haven't been down here since I was a child," Jix whispered.

"Why are we whispering?" Abby Gayle asked.

Speaking in a normal tone, Jix replied, "That's just what you do in a spooky basement."

"Oh."

Originating from numerous electrical boxes on the wall, wiring crisscrossed a low, unfinished ceiling like county roads on a map; snaking pipes represented main highways and a network of ductwork mimicked interstates.

Air permeated with dirt, dust, and time hung in the underground room like humidity on a summer day down South. Abby Gayle squeezed the flashlight Eva had suggested would come in handy.

A chilling spookiness filled a void left by the absence of noise or activity. Jix smoothed her hair rooted in a tingling scalp.

For lack of an immediate plan, Jix blurted out the first thought that surfaced. "There should be a staircase somewhere."

"There." Abby Gayle swept the dimly lit room with a spindly flashlight beam, focusing on steps partially hidden by a hefty support column.

"Let's start with the stairs. There may be an enclosed space underneath we should check. We can work our way from there back to here."

On the way, they stopped to inspect an obsolete incinerator. Presently, trash from the units above tossed down the incinerator chute landed in a dumpster. An overhead retractable door covered the opening. The door was firmly closed and locked. Satisfied there was nothing amiss, they continued toward the stairs.

"This place is a maze." Abby Gayle looked around. "A creepy maze," she whispered, placing the flashlight under her chin and upwards across her face. The fiery beam cast shadows juxtaposed by highlights to cause a distorted, skull-like appearance. "A crreeepy maze," she said in a ghoulish voice.

"Oh, stop it," Jix groaned. She didn't scare easily, but considering what they might find, she preferred staying on a positive note.

Abby Gayle laughed as she walked toward the freight elevator.

Jix shook a folding metal screen shielding the elevator's wide door and discovered it locked, just as Eva had said. A careful examination revealed no signs the gate had been jimmied or disturbed.

Old furniture, boxes, sleds, bicycles, tricycles, a refrigerator, and a mini pool table piled high in a dark corner caught their attention. "People move and leave things behind. This could have accumulated over many years," Jix concluded. They moved a few things around to better view items stacked against the wall.

"Trunks," Jix said. "Shine the light over here. Look, here are four or five old trunks. Let's see if there's anything in them. I see two camelbacks that I am definitely interested in if they've been abandoned by tenants."

They lifted a chair and a magazine rack off the trunks and slid them under an overhead bulb for better viewing. The two smaller trunks were locked. Two medium-sized trunks were packed with paintings, picture frames, books, and baby clothes. A large camelback held half-a-dozen rolls of wallpaper stored in tubes.

Abby Gayle lifted one of the smaller trunks. "Let's set them aside so we won't have to move them again. Eva may be glad to get them out of here."

Moving past the castoffs, the women inspected a row of flimsy, makeshift storage units constructed from two-by-fours and chicken wire. "Looks like individual storage for seldom used items." Jix noted a few of the ten-by-ten-foot enclosures were padlocked. Abby Gayle flashed the light beam over the contents inside the fencing.

"Bicycles," Jix mumbled.

They inspected spaces packed with dusty, discarded furniture, outgrown toys, and camping paraphernalia; a few spaces were empty.

Jix suddenly spotted something out of place. "What is that?" She moved to a support column and brushed the toe of her shoe against the base. Abby Gayle flashed the beam on her foot. Jix leaned down and picked up a playing card...the queen of hearts.

"It could have fallen out of something long ago," stated the person with the flashlight.

Jix turned the card over. "It's shiny...new."

It was, indeed, Abby Gayle agreed. She scanned the floor with a tiny spotlight, darting about like a mouse on the run.

"There's another." Jix eyed a jack of spades inside a fenced area. A flimsy, rectangular door made from strips of wood with wire stretched over it was unsecured. Jix opened it, and they stepped inside.

"Someone reasoned that padlocking the door is not much protection. Just a deterrent, I suppose." Abby Gayle shined the light beam on a chest of drawers. She moved the beam past then flashed it back to a card lying on top.

Jix picked up the six of diamonds. "This is like the trail of breadcrumbs. Either Marigold or Rossana must have left them. They must be leading us somewhere in particular." After a thorough search, they were satisfied there were no other cards.

Abby Gayle looked around. "The cards are in this unit. There must be something in here that someone wanted found."

There was nothing out of place nor a container or piece of furniture large enough to conceal a person, although a mattress leaning against the wall sparked their curiosity.

"Help me move this mattress away from the wall. Let's check behind it." Jix jammed the cards into her pocket. She angled the chest of drawers and slipped behind it. The overfilled space made it difficult to move around, much less move a mattress.

Abby Gayle propped the flashlight on the chest of drawers and aimed it for maximum illumination.

They worked in tandem to move items nearest the door to the outside of the enclosure. When there was adequate room, each grasped an end of the unwieldy mattress, and inched it from the wall so Abby Gayle could shine light behind it.

Struck by overwhelming shock, they stood aghast at what they'd uncovered.

"Rossana! Oh, no! Oh, no, no." Jix felt the tiny woman's wrist and neck for a pulse. Bowing her head, tears trickled down her cheeks.

Abby Gayle smoothed Rossana's hair. Choking back a sob she mumbled, "This can't be happening."

Clang! Clang! Clang!

A metal object drummed across the concrete floor. Earsplitting noise reverberated until whatever had fallen rolled to a stop.

Both jumped to their feet, hearts racing.

"Somebody's down here," Abby Gayle whispered. "Sounds like that came from near the freight elevator."

"It's hard to tell." Jix grabbed Abby Gayle's arm.

They ducked behind the furniture they'd moved out of the fenced area.

Footfall slapped the floor as the runner made a beeline for the elevator. Jix tried to catch the door before it closed, but was forced to snatch her fingers back to keep from crushing them. Gears engaged and the elevator launched.

"Drat! Drat! Drat!" exclaimed Jix, pounding her fists on the door.

The ladies stepped back to watch the floor indicator. They expected the elevator to stop on the first floor, assuming the intruder would leave the building by way of the front entrance.

Instead, the needle on the half-dial indicator moved past number one and number two and numbers three, four, and five...steadily it swung toward ten.

To the surprise of the sleuthsome twosome, the indicator hand stopped on the ninth floor.

Chapter Seven

"So, let me get this straight," Bill Haynes untied his robe and tossed it on the back of a chair, ran his thumbs around the elastic waistband on his plaid boxers, and then sat down on the bed and waited for his wife to clarify her statements. "Eva discovered Sonya injured and Marigold and Rossana missing. Then you and Abby Gayle found Rossana in the basement the police had already searched."

"Right." Jix nodded. She sat at her dressing table removing what was left of makeup applied at the start of the day. "And someone was in the basement when we found her, but we didn't know. We may have never known, but whoever was there knocked over this thingamabob. We found an iron cylinder when Detective Bird returned with her crew and the paramedics."

She brushed her hair with rapid strokes. "It had to be a man. A tall man…the runner took long strides, judging by the length of time it took to get to the elevator. And he wore boots. Only heavy boots would make the sound we heard."

"Astute observation, my dear." He was impressed with his

wife's keen ability to detect the unapparent. Bill fluffed his pillow, swung his feet onto the bed, and scooted under the comforter. "And Rossana? What about Rossana?"

Bill watched and waited.

She dipped her finger into a jar of wrinkle cream, leaned closer to the mirror, and puffed her cheeks like a hamster storing food. Rhythmically, the fifty-two-year-old grandmother moved the air bubble from cheek to cheek, back and forth, back and forth. Once she'd toned her facial muscles, she opened her mouth to form an elongated O, then closed and opened like a fish. Eyebrow raises and tiny-circle finger-massages completed the ritual.

"Well, that's the best part of all this so far," targeting fine lines with the silky cream, she answered. "I thought she was dead…I couldn't find a pulse. We had just found her when the intruder distracted us, so I hadn't had time to thoroughly assess the situation. From that point on things moved rapidly. To save time we didn't wait for the elevator to come back to the basement but took the stairs to the first floor, went into Eva's apartment, and called for help…and I called Detective Bird. It was from the ambulance crew I learned Rossana was—is—alive. Barely, but she is alive. She is such a neat, tiny, little bundle of a person. I think she once told us she is only four-foot-ten. She couldn't weigh more than ninety pounds soaking wet." Jix chuckled, as a flashback of Rossana over the years tugged at her heartstrings.

Bill turned off the bedside lamp on his side and hoped his wife would come to bed soon. "And what about Sonya? What's the latest word?" He closed his eyes and relished retreat from what had been a busy day.

"Still in a coma, but stable. They are optimistic she'll regain consciousness." Jix tidied up things on the dresser before turning off the other bedside lamp and sinking into the mattress.

When she closed her eyes, a message surged throughout her

body that this day was over. Her brain requested overtime.

"Oh, while I'm thinking about it, Newt Cochran is coming tomorrow to paint this room. They are going to move the furniture to the hallway and cover the carpet in here."

He didn't comment.

"Remember? I showed you the paint samples. Lilac with white trim." She folded back the comforter and turned toward him when he still didn't answer. "Bill."

"I hear you. If lilac doesn't work, you promised we'd paint over it with that royal blue I liked." He didn't care what color they ended up with as long as he wasn't the painter. He did, nevertheless, like for his preferences to be considered.

"The blue is too dark. You're going to love the lilac. It's soft and soothing and something we've never had before." She paused. "I don't remember ever painting a room lilac." It occurred to her there was probably a good reason why she'd never chosen the pastel color.

Jix continued, "Anyway, the Cochrans will be here before you leave in the morning. Please get Newt started on the room, and Carol will keep an eye on things as the day goes on. He and his son, Hal, are supposed to move the furniture back; it may be late in the day before the paint is dry. Thank goodness Carol's off work and not on call tomorrow because Mother and I have to be at Eva's at eight for the tenant's meeting and someone needs to be here to supervise. Abby Gayle is picking us up at seven-thirty. Newt should be here around nine."

"I'll get them started. What about trunks? Does Earl know what needs to be done? I can go to work after lunch if that will help. It's the middle of the month and things are slow at the office. Newt may need an extra hand moving furniture."

"Oh, honey, that would be great! I have two trunks to deliver on Friday…they're ready. The little tin trunk painted green is next up. If you build a tray for it that would be a step in the right direction."

"Will do. You shouldn't be long at this meeting, should you?" he asked.

"I plan to be back by lunch, but who knows? I'm going to the hospital, and Mother made an appointment with the Fairmont Foundation's Clifford or Bryson Purefoy to get an explanation as to what they are up to. And Waldo. We must contact Waldo." She hesitated before adding, "I don't know why, but I want to talk to Marigold's right-hand man."

"Aaron Williams?"

"Yes. He may know something about all this. I don't know what, I just know I keep coming back to him as I search my thoughts for who was in the basement. He's tall, and he has work boots. But then again, I'm not certain he is able to run. He has arthritis or a bad back or something."

Bill, who generally resisted being involved anytime he could avoid it didn't comment on Aaron; he hardly knew the man. "Ask Abby Gayle and your mother to help. Maybe one or both can make the hospital visits. I can call Waldo in the morning. I'll need a phone number." Bill adjusted his pillow and closed his eyes.

Silence blanketed the room.

For her mother's sake, Jix had suppressed doubts as to a positive outcome for Marigold. She could be honest with Bill.

"I'm worried sick about Marigold," Jix uttered a broken sob.

Bill rolled over and put his arm around her.

Before he could speak, his sweetheart's emotions bubbled over, "This is frustrating and confusing. Why would the Foundation sell Fairmont Manor? Why would anyone harm Marigold? What will happen to all the tenants if they have to leave? Why would whoever was hiding in the basement take the elevator to the ninth floor?"

"The vacant floor..." Bill mumbled. He tucked the sheet under her chin.

"Yes. The vacant floor. Why wouldn't someone escaping

leave through the front entrance? It was the nearest exit."

"Well, I'm glad you didn't take it upon yourself to search the ninth floor. Sweetheart, I'm telling you. Stay out of this, and let law enforcement do their job."

Absorbed in thought, selective hearing—that quality of convenience that allows one to hear only what they choose to hear—kicked in. "After finding Rossana neither Abby Gayle nor I were thinking clearly. Maybe we should have taken the stairs to the ninth floor. We may have been able to catch whoever was hiding." She directed her comment more to herself than to her husband.

"Oh, no! No! You did right by getting help. I want you to let Detectives Bird and Martino unravel all this." He reached for her hand and folded his around it, "Will you?"

"Prob'ly not," she said under her breath. "I wonder where Marigold is tonight. Is she frightened? Is she safe? Is she even alive?"

He searched for the right words. "Sweetheart, we mustn't allow ourselves to believe for anything other than a good outcome. Marigold is clever, and she is resourceful. She's strong-willed and accustomed to getting her way."

Jix mulled over his words and gained comfort from the truth he'd spoken. "I've just eliminated Aaron Williams as a suspect. Anyone who knows her personally would never risk becoming Marigold Fairmont's personal vendetta. It has to be someone who is unaware of who they are dealing with."

He kissed the tip of her nose. "That's right, honey. Marigold can take care of herself."

Chapter Eight

The following morning, a series of unexpected occurrences propelled the Haynes and their friends into a frenzy.

Abby Gayle had accepted an invitation to breakfast, issued by Carol when they'd talked on the phone the night before. She arrived an hour earlier than originally planned with high hopes the coffee was ready, and a dozen freshly baked, heavenly scented, cinnamon rolls from Snowden's Bakery.

Earl called to say he had a flat tire, and would Jix send someone to pick him up, then stop by Tidwell's Garage to drop the tire off…and get him to work on time.

Margee lost her glasses and enlisted the help of the entire household to search for them, only to locate the specs in her housecoat pocket, thirty minutes after the fruitless search began.

The Cochrans called to say they had been delayed, and it would be noon before they could start the painting project. Rescheduling was out of the question as they were booked solid for a month. Bill volunteered to clear the room, so they could get on with painting as soon as they arrived. That plan resulted in a plea to Abby Gayle's husband, Austin, for help.

Tall, good-natured, fair-haired Austin Kamp's job as a truck driver often kept him away on lengthy trips. Fortunately, he was home and willing to help Bill unload the bedroom, so the painters could finish and reload the room by bedtime. Austin's willingness awarded him the additional task of rescuing Earl and delivering him to his Trunk Doctor duties.

Dinah stumbled over a stuffed Winnie-the-Pooh and bumped her chin. After much consoling, the toddler was assured that Winnie was sorry and would never, ever intentionally assault a child.

The next crisis topped the Winnie confrontation. After filling the machine with water, Carol absentmindedly sat the coffee pot on the countertop rather than on the coffeemaker and ten minutes later returned to find twelve cups of coffee had freely flowed every place except where it should have.

Eva called seeking reassurance that Marigold would be found and the tenants meeting would go well. Ample support came from those who could have used a bit of comforting themselves.

Willowdean, the mostly-beagle, was the only one present that wasn't zipping around like a wound-up toy. Sensing an air of drama, she laid low under the dining room table with plans to hunker down until things grew calmer.

At a quarter till eight, Jix, Abby Gayle, and Margee headed to Eva's, leaving Bill and Carol in charge of the Cochrans and the lilac transformation.

The women arrived at Fairmont Manor to find a dozen or more tenants lingering in the foyer or mingling inside Eva's apartment.

The resident manager greeted the ladies with an announcement. "I've invited Detective Bird to join us and break the news to the group about Marigold, Rossana, and Sonya. I don't know what to tell them, and everyone is anxious to know what has happened. At the last minute, I called, and she came right over."

"She may have been on her way to work anyway," Abby Gayle reasoned.

Jix pulled Eva aside to repeat a discussion she, her mother, and Abby Gayle had in the car on their way there. "Eva, we're thinking that it might be a good idea to delay discussing the letter with the tenants. This is, of course, entirely up to you."

Margee expressed her opinion to delay. "Until we have more information, telling them about the letter is premature. Jix and I are to meet with Bryson Purefoy at eleven-thirty this morning. Come with us, Eva. Abby Gayle is coming too. There is power in numbers."

Abby Gayle nodded. "Once you know more about the Foundation's intentions, you can call another meeting."

Eva pondered their advice. "That's a good plan. I'd like to talk to Bryson's grandfather. I'll meet you at his office." Dread sprouted wings and fluttered off Eva's shoulder.

"I will wait. The news of Marigold and the possibility they may lose their home is a lot at once." She still reeled from the previous day's double whammy.

A few stragglers joined the others, including Avonelle Bird who'd been the last to arrive. Following apologies for cramped quarters, Eva suggested they sit or stand wherever there was space.

Juliet Pratt, glowing baker of a sour cream coffee cake drizzled with icing and toasted pecans, had taken charge of circulating the cake and coffee. The group had downed the first pot and waited for a second pot to brew.

After introductions, Eva called the meeting to order. "Many of our tenants work and are unable to attend this morning. We may have another meeting soon, perhaps at night so more residents can attend." She paused for latecomer Cathy Kessler.

Once Cathy had greeted everyone and parked herself on the arm of the sofa, Eva resumed. "Detective Bird of the Brookline Criminal Investigation Unit is here to speak to us concerning

Marigold Fairmont."

Eva looked into faces masked with concern, intensified by the words 'criminal investigation'.

"Several of you have inquired as to Miss Fairmont's whereabouts and as to recent events in general. Perhaps the detective can shed some light. So let's welcome Detective Avonelle Bird." A light spattering of applause met the policewoman's smile.

"Good morning to everyone. I know you are all concerned for your neighbor and friend. At this point, we don't have a lot of information as to the disappearance of Miss Fairmont and…"

"Disappearance!" Eddie Devlin sprang to his feet. The eighty-year-old, eighth floor resident who bore a striking resemblance to a leprechaun asked what others were wondering, "What do ya mean disappearance? Pray tell, how do ya go 'bout disappearin'?"

Bird held her up hand. "If you'll bear with me, I'll tell you what I know. It has only been twenty-four hours, and we are gathering facts and following leads."

Juliet Pratt cast a look toward Mr. Devlin that withered him like a thirsty petunia. He cleared his throat as he eased down on the sofa, steadying himself with a cane. Cathy Kessler leaned over and patted his shoulder before returning Juliet's unsolicited reprimand.

The detective continued.

"Miss Fairmont is not in her apartment. No one we have spoken to saw her leave or knows where she has gone."

To no surprise of those present, Mrs. Lockhart—third floor, apartment 3-B—teared up, blew her nose on a tissue, and dabbed at her eyes with a lace hanky.

Dan Pratt, as grouchy as his wife had predicted, spoke. "Do you suspect foul play? Where are Rossana and Sonya? They should know where Marigold is."

Bird offered little information other than both women were in the hospital. Emotions ranging from sadness to shock stirred a wave of chatter that washed over the room. Ebony Anderton comforted her wheelchair-bound son Troy. Sonya sometimes sat with him while his mother ran errands.

Jack and Inez Weaver, fourth floor residents, asked if there had been a break-in. Avoiding a direct answer, Bird assured them preventative measures were in place; a police officer patrolled the building and another monitored the front entrance.

Once the initial shock wore thin, conversation flowed more casually. The detective mingled and spoke individually with many of the residents.

Conversing with those present garnered no additional information, as no one had seen or heard anything out of the ordinary.

Juliet sliced the last of the cake and divvied it up among a few takers. Cathy gathered paper cups and dropped them down the garbage chute; Allison Meyers—fourth floor, apartment 4-A—asked to be excused as she had an appointment, and Rick Rutgers—seventh floor, apartment 7-B—suggested to Jix, after Avonelle Bird had left, that someone should contact Belinda Watson's boys if they were interested in locating secret passages or ways to get out of the building unnoticed.

Chapter Nine

Young Purefoy Junior towered over the ladies at six-foot-three. Flirty dimples emerged when he flashed a mouthful of pearly whites. The elusive little craters deepened when he laughed and played peek-a-boo when he talked.

"Nice to see you Mrs. Fairmont," he smiled at Margee. "And you ladies, as well. What can I do for you this fine morning?" He scooted behind a solid-wood executive desk and sank into a swivel chair. The ladies took chairs facing Bryson Purefoy.

"Is your grandfather here today?" Eva asked.

"No, he isn't. Grandfather is retiring soon due to health issues. I'll assume his duties." He leaned back in the plush leather chair and laced his fingers. Bryson had joined the Foundation less than a year earlier to manage investments and help with administrative tasks.

Eva passed the letter to him. "To say I was surprised to receive this is a vast understatement. No one has spoken to me concerning any changes at Fairmont Manor."

Stone-faced, he looked at the letter. Handing the notice back to Eva, he chose his words carefully. "With all due respect, Mrs.

Helton, we are under no obligation to discuss decisions with you. You are an employee of sorts."

Jix bit her lip. She responded in the politest tone she could manage, "Common decency is all that is needed to compel you to inform Mrs. Helton early on of a matter of this magnitude. She hasn't suggested you are expected to consider her opinion. Actually, this is news to us as well. Is Marigold Fairmont aware that you've thrown her out of her home?"

"Why don't you ask her?" he retorted. A smug smile summoned both delightful dimples.

Margee Fairmont looked the fair-haired fellow squarely in the eye, and, as ladylike as her temperament would allow, proceeded to state the facts in rapid sequence.

"Mr. Purefoy, as you may or may not know, my husband David Fairmont was a member of the Board of Trustees for forty years, as I am presently an active trustee. This is a family foundation. I am certain you are fully aware of this, but in case you've forgotten, or you've been misinformed, may I reiterate? This is a *family foundation*."

With fire in her eyes, she scooted to the edge of the chair.

"Marigold's parents set up the Foundation to be funded primarily by rental revenues from Fairmont Manor. After operating expenses and maintenance, remaining funds are distributed to various charities...it's been this way since day one; still is today, and is likely to be throughout eternity. This is a well-structured, legal, non-profit corporation. I don't know what is going on or what your goal may be. The one thing I do know with certainty is that Fairmont Manor can never be sold or disposed of in any form or fashion without the approval and consent of the Board of Trustees, as well as the president of the foundation; the honorable, loved, and respected Marigold Catherine Joelle Fairmont."

Her eyes bore into the young man like lasers, deflating his ego. "And to the best of my knowledge, Miss Marigold Catherine

50

Joelle Fairmont has not consented or approved of even so much as a discussion of vacating or selling the property, much less a notice to do so." She raised her chin and looked down her nose with an air of finality.

Margee had clout. And she'd used it masterfully. Jix, Abby Gayle, and Eva had to restrain from applauding. Jix's soft-spoken, gentle-natured mother's stance against an unscrupulous man had been a memorable, standing- ovation performance. The woman had pinned the ears back on a pretentious, self-absorbed man who dared to waste perfectly good, dazzling, heart-palpitating dimples.

The meeting ended abruptly. They left knowing little more than they'd known when they arrived. On the way to the parking lot, Jix presented a valid point.

"Now I understand why they told you to close two entire floors, Eva. Losing income from twelve units reduces vital revenue the Foundation depends on to fulfill obligations to its charities. Bryson has overstepped his bounds and he has to be stopped before more damage is done. Immediately repairs must be addressed, resolved, and all apartments rented."

Abby Gayle added, "He's smart enough to know he cannot do anything with a building he doesn't own. There is more to this than meets the eye. And it will be interesting to discover if his plans included assaulting and kidnapping women."

"Oh, my goodness!" Margee's hand flew to her cheek. "I've known Clifford Purefoy half my lifetime. Clifford married Yolanda Fairmont who passed away years ago. Eric, their only child, is Bryson's father. Eric and his latest wife live in Hawaii, last I heard. I can't believe Clifford would be a part of anything that would harm the foundation or Marigold. I'm baffled as to what Bryson is doing."

Margee explained that the Foundation was created by Marigold's parents to ensure she had a home for as long as she chose to live at Fairmont Manor, and to leave a philanthropic legacy.

"I'll call," Margee said, "and enlighten the other board members. Charles Pennington, the Foundation's attorney, will look into this." She sighed. "Carol will have lunch ready. I'm anxious to find out if Bill was able to reach Waldo."

"Hopefully, the Cochrans are painting," Jix said. "Eva, I'd like to talk with Belinda Watson's boys. Do you know what time they get home from school? Are they in an after-school program?"

"I keep an eye on the older boys the afternoons they don't have football practice or other activities. Jennalee and Jerry stay with me every afternoon until Belinda gets home...usually before five-thirty, so I only have the children for two hours or less. I help Belinda when I can. She works hard to provide for her children."

Abby Gayle asked, "How old are these kids?" They had reached the cars. Margee slid into the driver's seat when Jix opened the truck door.

Eva leaned against the fender of her car parked beside Jix. She dug around in her purse to retrieve her keys. "James will soon be fourteen, Jonathan is twelve, Jerry is ten, and Jennalee is eight. They are well-behaved kids—very inquisitive, energetic children—especially the two older boys. I've grown quite attached to them."

"Shall Abby Gayle and I come at four to chat with them?" Jix checked with her friend. "If you want to come."

"Sure. I've been gone since daybreak. May as well make a day of it. I'll go home for lunch, check on Austin, and wash a load of laundry. I'll meet you at Eva's."

"Good. We'll see you at four, Eva. Scoot over, Mom. I hope things are running more smoothly at home than when we left this morning," she joked.

Chapter Ten

Jix glanced at the kitchen clock shaped like half an apple with seeds for numerals. Straight up and down one o'clock.

"Is your Dad still here?" She asked her daughter.

"He's in the den with Dinah," Carol answered. "Lunch is ready." She had makings for tacos and fajitas on the table. "Dad!" she yelled. "Soup's on!"

Margee washed her hands at the sink, poured a glass of tea, and pulled out a chair. "Looks good, sweetheart. Thanks for cooking," she surveyed the food before her. "Are the Cochrans here?"

"Arrived an hour or so ago." Carol filled the glasses with ice and added a couple of cubes to her grandmother's glass.

Bill choo-choo-chooed in with Dinah atop his shoulders.

"Train station ahead," he announced as he slid the laughing little girl down and into her highchair. He gave Jix a loving pat on her backside and a peck on the cheek and took his place at the table.

Everyone grew quiet and closed their eyes as Bill blessed the food.

"'men," Dinah said, reaching for chunks of meat and veggies nestled in a suction plate stuck to the highchair tray.

"How'd things go?" he asked, as Jix and Carol passed the food.

Jix highly touted her mother's stance against an arrogant, dimpled pipsqueak. "Mama gave Bryson Purefoy a tongue lashing that had him cowering like a scolded pup."

Slightly embarrassed and just a tad proud, Margee recapped the morning's events. "I'll call Charles Pennington and see what he has to say about all this. He'll be at lunch now. I'll call soon as he returns. We'll put a stop to this and get those repairs underway so the units can be rented. This is ridiculous. If any good comes out of all this, it will be that Bryson has been exposed before doing irreversible damage."

Bill considered that damage done might not be reversible but kept his comments to himself in an effort to remain as uninvolved as possible.

Jix announced her plans to visit the Watson children. She then asked how Earl was coming along with trunk work. Bill reported what he knew and brought everyone up to date on activity in the upstairs bedroom.

"Did you reach Waldo?" Jix asked.

"I did. Finally. That fellow gets around; I had to chase him down. He became distraught, as we all are, when I told him that Marigold is missing. He said he would leave immediately and be here in a few hours."

"Where is he?" Carol asked. She spooned macaroni and cheese leftover from the night before into Dinah's dish.

"Savannah," Bill answered. "Since he'll arrive around supper time, Waldo suggested we meet at the barbeque joint over on Halstead Street at six. Neither of us could remember the name of the place."

"Halstead Street Bar-B-Q," Carol and Margee said collectively.

"That sounds right." Bill had thought it was called the Pork

Palace. He continued, "I told Waldo if that wasn't agreeable with everyone, I'd let him know. Can we all make it? I've decided not to go to the office today. Moving furniture was a bigger job than I'd anticipated. We have too much furniture, Jix. Without Austin's help, I'd still be working on it."

"Duly noted," Jix said in between bites. In her opinion, they had plenty of room for more furniture.

"Dad, make excuses for me..." Carol said, "...but give Waldo my kindest regards. He's such a nice man."

Margee added, "And excuses for me. I'd love to see Waldo, but I have plans to go to play practice at the community theatre."

"Well, I'll go to Eva's at four then meet you and Waldo at six. Abby Gayle will be with me. She can call Austin if they want to join us. I'll work with Earl until time to go to Eva's. Maybe I should check in on Newt and Hal first."

Bill cautioned, "He said not to."

"Not to what?"

"Go up there until they're finished." Bill spooned sautéed peppers and onions onto his plate.

Jix froze, her fork suspended in motion. "You've always claimed to be head of this household. Did I miss something? When did Newt take over?"

Bill laughed, "He didn't say not to go upstairs; he asked if we would wait until the room is painted and the furniture is back in place. He likes to make a big deal out of the "reveal," as he put it."

"Oh. Well, I guess that makes sense. However, we won't be here when they finish," Jix said.

Carol layered a tortilla with strips of marinated flank steak. "And by the time you see the big reveal, just like Elvis, Newt and son will have left the building."

Chapter Eleven

"Are we in trouble?" A stray strand of chestnut-brown hair rested on James Watson's furrowed forehead. Shaded by the brim of a baseball cap, knitted brows arched over the lanky adolescent's hazel eyes. He jammed his hands in his jeans pockets and shifted from one foot to the other.

Shoulder high to his brother, Jonathan Watson provided a defense before there was an accusation, "We didn't do nothing." He folded his arms against a striped tee shirt, prepared to stand his ground.

Suppressing a smile, Jix assured the boys they were not being accused of anything. "I heard you are the go-to when it comes to…let's call them secret…passages in this old building. Ever go exploring in your spare time?"

"Might have," the elder brother confessed.

The self-appointed defender rose to the occasion once more. "We didn't steal nothing, we didn't break nothing, and we didn't do nothing."

Abby Gayle put her hands on her hips. "Nobody said you did, but if you keep on running your mouth, we may decide you have something to hide by protesting too much. Don't talk yourself into a problem you don't need."

"Shut up!" James said to his brother.

"Okay, listen, you two," Jix said. "We have a little time before Miss Eva and your sister and brother return from the park. We're not accusing you of anything. We know you've explored the crooks and crannies of this building, and we need your help. Have you heard that Miss Marigold is missing?" Jix knew immediately they didn't know. She hoped she wasn't the one in trouble.

James answered, "Nobody tells us anything. I overhead some talk, but I don't know details."

"Well," Jix led them from the kitchen where they'd finished a snack to the sofa, "Let me tell you what we know. But first, I need your word that you will keep all this to yourself. Let's play detective and figure out how someone would get out of this building without going out the front door?"

Jix sat on the end of Eva's slipcovered couch; Abby Gayle sunk into an overstuffed side chair.

The brothers communicated non-verbally. Eye contact that was meaningless to the ladies transmitted emotional and nonverbal messages between the boys. James broke the silence.

"Well, of course the fire escape. If a person hid in something, even though someone would have to open the front door, they could get out without being seen. But…" He dropped his head. James' leg jiggled nervously. He looked at his brother. Jonathan nodded.

"But we found this one place that I don't think anybody knows about. Miss Marigold may know. Mama said she's lived here all her life."

"Place?" He had Jix and Abby Gayle's attention. Abby Gayle asked, "What do you mean by place?"

"I don't know what it is. One Saturday afternoon, we stumbled on it. There wadn't nothing to do; it was raining so we couldn't go to the park. Mama was at work, Jerry and Jennalee were at Miss Eva's, so we decided to poke around the basement. This old building is a great place to spend a rainy day. If you can't find nothing else to do, you can ride the elevator till somebody tells you to stop."

Jonathan piped up, "We didn't hurt nothing. We just found this thing by accident."

Jix and Abby Gayle's curiosity ran rampant. "Can you show us?' Jix asked.

"I reckon." James stood. Jonathan tugged on his shirttail. "What?"

"We need to take a couple of flashlights. 'Member that bulb is burned out."

"He's right." James started toward the desk. "Miss Eva keeps a flashlight in the bottom desk drawer."

"There's one in the basement. I know where it is." Blue-eyed, freckled-faced Jonathan had rested his case and become more cooperative. "Let me push the elevator button. It's my turn," the typical twelve-year-old said to his brother.

"Is not."

"Is too."

"Is not."

Ignoring the debate, Abby Gayle suggested they leave a note for Eva in case she returned before they did. Jonathan ran to the desk to get a pad and pen.

Chapter Twelve

By the time the elevator glided to a stop, the Watson boys were leading the expedition with the fervor of Lewis and Clark.

James stepped into the basement and went directly to the electrical switches, flipping the right ones as if he'd done so many times. Jonathan fetched an additional flashlight and instructed Jix and Abby Gayle to follow long-legged James.

"Jonathan stumbled over this, or we might not have found it," The four stood over a rectangular metal grate the size of a large manhole cover.

"Looks like a drain," Abby Gayle surmised.

Jonathan agreed. "That's what we thought at first, but when I looked at this thing…" he squatted and used the flashlight as a pointer, "…it reminded me of a handle on a bucket. See what I'm saying?"

Jix was impressed. "I do. Even though it is recessed, it looks like a handle. You have a keen eye. So, is it a lever? Did you try it?"

"Oh, yeah," chimed James. "Did we ever! Like to have scared us half to death." The boys laughed when they told how they'd been tempted to run up the stairs.

Jix took the flashlight from James, squatted, and examined the grate up close. "It isn't open like a drainage duct," she said to Abby Gayle, who'd leaned down to a get a better view.

Abby Gayle said to the youngsters, "What happened when you pulled the band?"

"Stand back," James said. "Way back," Jonathan added.

Jix and Abby Gayle stepped back.

The older boy straddled the grate, wiggled his fingers underneath the metal rod, and braced with his legs. James gave it a hearty jerk and, in an instant, jumped aside.

To the amazement of the women, heavy metal gears rumbled. The grate retracted like a pocket door. Within seconds, the metal plate beneath it slid open to reveal a large, gaping, black hole.

The four knelt down to peer into the abyss.

"Do you know what's down there?" Abby Gayle asked. Both boys answered, "It's a tunnel."

"Tunnel?" Jix and Abby Gayle questioned. "Did you go in it?"

"Yeah, but not far. It was scary down there, and we decided to turn around. There's a ladder to the bottom. And I think there's lights because when we came out, I saw a switch just inside here," he leaned into the opening to feel for a light switch.

"That's what I told you. The bulb's burned out. Over from the switch there's a light bulb," Jonathan repeated.

"James, if one of us can reach the fixture, we can replace the bulb, assuming it's a standard light bulb," Jix said, standing to stretch her back and legs.

"All I need is to go down a few rungs on the ladder; then I think I can reach over and get it. Somebody'll have to hold the flashlight so I can see."

James entered the tunnel with Eva's flashlight in one hand, and a grip on the ladder with the other. Once he'd located the fixture, he passed the flashlight up to Jix, who lay prone on the concrete floor with her upper torso in the hole. With flashlights in both hands, she aimed the beams so James could see to loosen the bulb. Within minutes, he triumphantly held a standard, hundred-watt light bulb for all to see.

Jonathan, who had inventoried every drawer and shelf in the basement on more than one rainy day, knew where spare bulbs were kept. When he selected a bulb, he also noted the apple, peanut butter sandwich, and candy bar he'd left in the drawer the day before were gone.

James replaced the useless one and *voilà*! There was light.

Jix dangled her feet into the hole and felt for the rungs. With calculated intent, she inched her way down. The Watson brothers went next. Abby Gayle brought up the rear; she ventured to guess it was twenty or more feet to the bottom. Midway, she wondered if they should have gone down one at a time. No one had considered whether the ladder could bear the weight of four at once.

Illumination from the fixture high above shed sparse light on the path before them once they'd reached the tunnel floor. Abby Gayle swung the flashlight from side to side, noting what she estimated to be an eight-foot wide passageway.

"It's narrow," she drew attention to the closeness of the opening. "This must be an air duct." She focused the light on an open, round pipe overhead.

The walls and floor were nothing more than packed dirt. Wooden beams supported what she guessed to be eight-foot ceilings strung with interspersed, non-functioning light bulbs. James reasoned that all lights were on one circuit. Someone in a hurry must have forgotten to turn them off and they had all burned out.

Abby Gayle started counting steps from the ladder into the tunnel. After two hundred, she lost count. "We've come at least sixty or seventy yards," she said. "I think we are going west of Fairmont Manor. I'm trying to figure where we would be if we were on the streets overhead."

James commented, "It may not come out anywhere. Maybe it's just a place to hide."

"It's spooky down here." Jonathan remembered why they had turned back before. He counted on there being safety in numbers.

"James will have a lot to write in his journal tonight," Jonathan said, following close behind his brother.

Jix asked over her shoulder, "You keep a journal?"

As the line proceeded through pitch-black darkness illuminated by two cone-shaped flashlight beams, James shyly remarked that he liked to record his adventures, limited as they were.

"Ow!" Jonathan yelled and jumped about.

"What?" Jix spun around. Abby Gayle shined the light on the boy. "Something ran across my foot. I felt it!"

Both women searched with the lights. "May have been a rat," Jix said. Her skin crawled. A dawning realization crept over her that she and her best friend were casually burrowing through a tunnel like groundhogs and gophers—a tunnel that could deliver them to an unpleasant fate.

She factored in that she had assumed responsibility for someone else's children, and not a soul in the world knew they were underground. Should there be a search, it would appear the four had disappeared off the face of the earth. Jix swallowed hard. Then she remembered the purpose for tunneling to the unknown. Marigold. She had to find Marigold.

"You all right?" Abby Gayle asked.

"Yes. Let's keep going."

"Want me to take the lead for a while? I feel like the donkey's tail back here."

"No. I'm following my nose," Jix joked.

"We're following you. Now, back to James and his journal," Abby Gayle sought to assure the boys that all was well, even though she didn't have the foggiest notion as to whether things were well or not.

Jonathan proudly stated, "Someday James is going to be a famous mystery writer. We can say we knew him when." They all laughed.

Abby Gayle predicted that James had a ready-made agent in his brother Jonathan. She knew a wheeler-dealer when she saw one.

Jix pretended, "Dream big, boys. Let's consider ourselves a research team. We're exploring tunnels to gather material for James the writer to turn into a cliffhanger mystery."

The mood brightened, and the brave band of adventurers continued a lengthy distance until Jix's flashlight beam bounced off something in their path. The surprised leader stopped abruptly, causing a pile up. Sandwiched boys untangled themselves; Abby Gayle stopped but not before smacking Jonathan's head with her flashlight.

"I'm sorry, so sorry for the pile up," Jix sought to make amends. "We've reached the end of the tunnel. There's a ladder just ahead. Light reflected off the metal and startled me."

Clever Jonathan quipped, "There's always light at the end of the tunnel."

Facing the exit, uncertainty as to what they might find topside sparred with burning curiosity. No one was anxious to forfeit safety in the tunnel for lurking danger. Nor did anyone want to settle for turning around and never knowing what was overhead.

Jix volunteered. "I'll climb up and see if we can get out."

Both Abby Gayle and James offered to go instead, but Jix insisted she go.

"If there's trouble, Abby Gayle, run. Get the boys back to Fairmont Manor, and call Detective Bird."

She took one flashlight; James held the other. Abby Gayle and Jonathan moved aside as Jix mounted the spindly rungs. It was too difficult to hold the flashlight while she climbed. She handed the torch to James.

"There has to be a way to open the hatch from inside," she mumbled.

James stood a few rungs below Jix. He targeted a bead on the metal door suspended over their heads. "Remember, the latch looks like a handle."

She had already spotted it. Lacing her fingers underneath the lever, she pulled. Rumbling like rocks rolling down a mountainside, the metal plate opened, and the grate above it folded back. Fresh air rushed in.

James climbed higher.

Jonathan and Abby Gayle started their ascent. Jix cautiously poked her head through the opening to eye level.

She trolled into pitch-blackness like a human periscope.

A pungent odor stung her nose.

"Whew!!" Jix stretched the neck of her tee shirt over her nose to filter the stench. There was no mistaking the odor. Nothing smells like cat litter.

"Where are we?" she exclaimed.

Chapter Thirteen

"Hand me the flashlight, James," Jix whispered over her shoulder.

She flashed the beam from end to end of what had all the features of a roomy closet.

"Meow!"

A huge, fluffy, cinnamon-colored cat with golden eyes stepped lithely from the shadows and politely greeted unexpected company with a head rub.

"Hello, kitty," she said.

A more thorough inspection of the area revealed a full litter box, a closed door, clothes hanging overhead, and three pair of men's shoes neatly lined in a row, a pair of work boots among them.

"We're in a closet," she said to the others, hanging on the ladder like grapes on a vine. "I assume no one is here, or they would have heard the grate open and would have investigated by now."

Jix climbed out and opened the closet door. Light spilled in as quickly as the cat darted out. The boys and Abby Gayle emerged from the hole and huddled closely behind Jix.

"Hello," she called.

"Jix, we need to stop and think. How would you react if you were napping on the couch and four strangers walked out of your closet? We are standing in someone's bedroom. It doesn't get much weirder than this."

"Duly noted. Even so, it stands to reason if anyone were here, they would have rushed in."

"Unless they are loading their shotgun," Abby Gayle supposed.

"Or calling the police," Jonathan whispered.

"Stay here with the boys. I'll look around."

Jix knocked on the door leading into the next room. Abby Gayle and the kids nosed about the bedroom; the brothers busily gathered clues.

"A man lives here," James announced when Jix returned. "There are only men's clothes in the closet, and there's three watches on the bureau, all mens."

Jonathan reported his observances, "There's shaving stuff in the bathroom and a girlie magazine on the rim of the bathtub."

Responding with a what-were-you-thinking expression, Jix asked, "You let them look at a girlie magazine?"

"Hey! They went in the bathroom. I respected their privacy," Abby Gayle filed the incident under no big deal and moved along. "We should get out before whoever lives here returns. Are we going back through the tunnel?"

The now familiar rumble of the tunnel doors rang throughout the house.

James explained, "The doors close after awhile. We tried to close them the day we found the tunnel but couldn't figure out how. Then, they closed themselves. The grate in the basement should be closed by now."

"I want to look at the outside of the house. Maybe we can determine how far we are from Fairmont Manor." Jix led the way to the front room.

Jonathan spotted a hat on a hall tree in the foyer. He took it down and fingered it thoughtfully. "James, remember when Mr. Williams gave us a ride to school the morning we missed the bus? This looks like the hat he wore."

James moved closer. "It is the same hat. I said it looked like a gangster's hat. I recognize this feather in the band. Cool!" He put it on his head.

"Mr. Williams? Are you talking about Aaron Williams who works for Miss Marigold?" Abby Gayle asked.

"Yeah. I don't know where he lives, but I know this is his hat."

"Well, now I think you also know where he lives. Let's look in the garage. He keeps Marigold's car." They traipsed through the kitchen.

"By the way, I fed the cat," Jix said. "Look for a bag of cat litter in the garage, and we'll leave a clean litter box."

The younger brother said, "There's litter and plastic bags in the closet in the bathroom. Wait on me, and I'll take care of it. We used to have a cat."

"You don't miss much, do you?" Jix chortled. She had enjoyed spending time with the Watson brothers. They were bright, well-mannered children.

Abby Gayle glanced at her wristwatch. "Whatever we do, we need to do it if you are meeting Waldo at six."

The garage was empty of vehicles of any kind. When they stepped out into the yard, Jix and Abby Gayle recognized the house they'd each driven past countless times over the course of many years, but neither had known who owned or lived in the house. The boys walked ahead as the women kept them in sight.

Meanwhile, back at Fairmont Manor, Belinda Watson had collected her younger children and left word for her two older sons to come straight home. The brothers would not tell her of the afternoon adventure. Their mother was not likely to believe it, anyway. The boys found it difficult to believe, and they were there.

Waldo had called to announce he was in town. Eva told him what little she knew and gave him phone numbers for Sonya's niece and Rossana's sister.

Eva Helton was dumbfounded when told of the discovery of the tunnel and where it led. "That has to be how they got out of the building, but why would Marigold tell anyone about the tunnel? That makes no sense. It would have been to her benefit to leave through a more traceable exit."

Abby Gayle speculated. "Unless whoever took them knew of the tunnel. Aaron Williams, for instance. He knew."

Eva verified that the old Greek Revival two-story on the corner of Baker and Boudreau Streets was Fairmont property where the handyman, chauffeur, escort, and jack-of-all trades resided.

When hearing that the cat was locked in the closet, Eva was concerned that Aaron had left in a hurry and perhaps unwillingly.

"The cat must have accidentally closed the door. Aaron loves that cat. He talks about her as if she were a child. He would never leave Nelda without food and extra litter if he planned to be away for any length of time," she said. "It doesn't sound to me as if Aaron planned to be gone long, if at all."

Chapter Fourteen

The aroma of sizzling barbeque sauce dripping off simmering meat onto red-hot hickory coals greeted diners. Waldo and Bill had ordered drinks by the time Jix parted with Abby Gayle and made her way through heavy traffic.

A hug for each of the men came with an apology for being late. She slid in the booth next to Bill and across from Marigold's beau. Tromping through a tunnel had left her tired, hungry, and ready for a break.

"So good of you to come, Waldo. We are stumped as to why this has happened and where Marigold is. Had she mentioned problems with anyone or anything recently?"

The portly man of average height with a band of wavy, gray hair reaching from ear to ear across the back of his shiny head leaned forward, propped his elbows on the table, and frowned. "No. I'm baffled. She didn't say anything to me about any trouble. Not too long ago…oh, maybe six months or so…she had a run in with a neighbor. For the life of me, her name escapes me. But as far as I know, nothing came of it. The woman moved and I heard no more about it."

A pony-tailed waitress dressed in a western shirt and painfully tight-fitting jeans slid a tray of drinks onto the table. They ordered food and Waldo instructed the young girl, who'd introduced herself as Ashley, to put everything on one ticket.

Waldo continued, "I've talked with the woman detective in charge. She didn't have much to tell. I'm to meet with her tomorrow. I called Eva. She gave me phone numbers for Sonya's niece and Rossana's sister. Never met Sonya's niece, but I know Marie, Rossana's younger sister. I've talked with both ladies since Bill called this morning."

Jix blurted out, "When we found her, we thought she was dead."

"Sonya?"

"No, Rossana. Abby Gayle and I found her in the basement. I didn't detect a pulse, but the paramedics were able to revive her."

Waldo leaned against the cushioned back of the booth and rested one leg on the seat. "Her sister said Rossana was lifeless when the paramedics started CPR. Marie talked about something called Lazarus' Syndrome. It's a very rare occurrence, but the way it was explained to me—not by Rossana's sister: I called a friend who's a doctor—nobody is certain as to what takes place, but one theory is that when CPR is administered, pressure builds up in the chest." He gestured with upturned palms slowly rising. "Once there are no more compressions, pressure relaxes and causes the heart to expand." He spread his hands apart. "This triggers the heart's electrical impulses that restart heartbeat."

Bill was amazed. "Wow! Sounds like a miracle in the making."

"I'm so relieved she is alive," Jix said, "and I'm anxious to talk with her. She knows who came in the apartment and assaulted Sonya, trashed the place, and took her and Marigold. She can tell us who did this, and she may know what has happened to Marigold."

Waldo was one step ahead. "Marie says Rossana has been unable to have visitors so far, not even the police; they are anxious to interview her. There's a police guard in the hallway outside the room. Marie tells me the doctors will allow a limited number of visitors tomorrow."

Bill speculated, "No doubt your friend Detective Bird will be first to talk with her. She may ask Rossana not to share information if doing so could jeopardize her investigation."

"She won't be first if we go tonight." Waldo's blue eyes twinkled. His neatly manicured mustache brushed the rim of a mug as pursed lips sipped coffee.

A what-is-that-smell look spread over Bill's face. **We?** If **we** go tonight?

The food arrived and was passed around, but after the waitress left, everyone sat still.

Jix, feeling the residuals of a hectic day catching up with her, softly inquired, "What do you have in mind, Waldo?"

"I'll tell you while we eat. Looks good. Dig in."

"Well, while we're mulling over crucial points of interest, we should consider that Aaron Williams and Marigold's car are missing too. And I want to tell you what I discovered this afternoon in the basement of Fairmont Manor. And Bryson Purefoy wants every tenant out of the apartment complex." She caught her breath, forked a bite of baked beans, and savored the smoky-flavored pintos marinated in tangy sauce.

"Oh, hell's bells." Bill straddled his plate with his elbows and plopped his head in his hands.

He had a strong feeling he was being sucked into something he had no desire to be part of.

Waldo chuckled and chewed at the same time. There were few men he respected more than peace-loving Bill Haynes.

Chapter Fifteen

Jix and Waldo polished a plan while Bill pretended not to listen. Their objective was to get into Rossana's hospital room undetected by the officer on duty. Marie was aware of the plan and doing her part at the hospital until the others arrived. Waldo called from his car phone to tell her they were on the way.

Marie waited fifteen minutes, and then, as instructed by Waldo, she carried her sister's dinner tray to the hallway and placed it on a fold-down shelf outside the door. She smiled and wiggled her derriere like a cat about to pounce on a catnip toy. A sweet smile and a hello to the policeman on duty, and she darted back inside.

Steve Solder, veteran cop of eighteen years, neared the end of his shift monitoring traffic going in and out of Rossana Ruiz' room. Since assigned to this case two days ago, the widower cop had become friendly with Marie Ruiz. Their conversations and her friendly presence helped to make each shift pass more quickly.

Waldo, Jix, and Bill exited the third-floor elevator and, two abreast with Bill dogging a step behind, began a long walk down the hospital corridor.

"Let's don't get in a hurry. Act casual," Waldo said, without moving his lips. They made a point of looking at the number on each door although the navy blue, uniformed officer was a dead giveaway as to their destination.

Without warning, Waldo stopped abruptly just short of Officer Solder…so abruptly Bill plowed into him, jumped back in an attempt to maintain balance, and knocked the dinner tray off the shelf.

"Oh, no!" Bill gasped. "Sorry. So sorry!"

"That's all right, honey," Jix sought to comfort him.

Once relieved of its load, the little ledge snapped shut with a bang. Plastic dishes bounced, clanged, and rolled in every direction. The tray struck the tiled floor like a clash of cymbals.

Marinara soaked strands of spaghetti stuck for a few seconds before sliding down the wall.

A runaway meatball hid underneath Officer Solder's folding chair. Another chased a cherry tomato catapulted from a bowl of lettuce, leaving a cucumber bedfellow behind.

A half-eaten dish of chocolate pudding splattered like bird droppings on a windshield. Little puddles of coffee beaded on the glassy-polished floor.

"What's happened?" Marie rushed out to investigate and immediately recognized her cue.

She franticly picked up dishes as fast as she could pluck them from the spill and thrust them to Officer Solder to hold while she gathered more.

"What? No! Wait!" he sputtered. Caught off guard, he cradled the messy dishes in the crook of his arm.

Unhappy with sticky food on his fingers and shirtsleeve, he stooped to grasp the tray that had finally landed upside down following a topsy-turvy, end-over-end tumble. After several attempts, while slipping and sliding in the spill, he cornered the tray, flipped it over, and plunked the messy dishes on it.

Doors up and down the hallway opened as patients and visitors came to investigate.

"Everything's fine. Stay inside. Just a little accident." Nurses rushed on the scene, instructing everyone to return to their rooms. To those in the hallway, they cautioned not to slip on the strewn mess.

Waldo flicked a stubborn strand of pasta off the wall, pushed the partially closed door open, and undetected, he and Jix ducked inside.

Bill backed away from the incident. He hoped not to be blamed, and reminded himself this sort of thing happened every time he ruled against his better judgment.

When Rossana saw Waldo and Jix, she burst into tears, extending her arms for Jix to fly into.

"Mr. Waldo!" The tiny woman's shaking arms wrapped around Waldo's neck. Familiar faces restored her sense of belonging.

Waldo leaned close to say, "Dear, sweet, Rossana, we don't have much time. We aren't supposed to be in here. Can you tell us briefly what happened? Who did this? Do you know where Marigold is?"

Jix sat down on the bed and held Rossana's hands. "Is the person who did this someone you know?" Jix saw the woman through welling tears. She leaned over and hugged her, so thankful to be talking with this kind soul she'd thought she would never speak to again.

"Yes," Rossana answered. "I'll save the details for later, but the person who burst into our home once lived on the eighth floor. Her name is Lisandra Judd."

"Bingo!" said Waldo. "That's the woman Marigold told me had accused her of trying to take some man she was dating. Marigold couldn't convince her that the man was only an acquaintance and nothing more."

Jix asked, "Where does the Judd woman live now? Why would

she become violent? Where could she have taken Marigold?"

"I don't know. I don't know why she did this or where she took Miss Marigold. She had this wild look in her eyes...and she had a long knife," her hands spread far apart. "A thin, sharp knife."

"A stiletto," Waldo said.

"No. No. Not a shoe. It was a sharp knife."

Waldo's mouth fell open to explain that a stiletto was the type of knife or dagger used, but words kept tumbling off Rossana's lips. She slung her arm, "And this woman we do not like threw the white turtle and hit Sonya! Poor Sonya!" Racked with sadness, she gasped for breath, sobbing uncontrollably as memory replayed the scene.

Jix and Waldo embraced the heartbroken woman offering comfort, telling her to rest, and promising they would find Marigold.

Marie rushed in, her dark eyes flashing an urgent warning, "You need to go. It's time for medications. I see the nurse at the end of the hall. I'll distract Steve until you can leave."

"Steve?" Jix asked.

"Officer Solder. He's the policeman on duty." Marie cracked the door open and quickly closed it. "They are cleaning in the hallway. That will provide cover. You must hurry."

Woeful good-byes accompanied promises to find Lisandra Judd. Jix recommended Rossana tell Detective Bird everything and vowed to come again the following day if visitors were allowed.

They retrieved Bill from a waiting room at the end of the corridor near the elevator. The trio located Waldo's car in the parking deck and piled in to discuss their findings on the way back to the restaurant where both Bill and Jix had left their vehicles.

"I'll call Abby Gayle as soon as I get home." Jix relied on her best friend to bring reason and practical solutions to situations.

Jix tended to be the more fearless of the two; Abby Gayle added forethought and prudence. Together, they were an unstoppable force.

Waldo slowed to a stop at an intersection. "I'll call Eva and see if I might stop by. She knows Lisandra Judd and may have a forwarding address. I'll stay in Marigold's apartment tonight if Eva has no objections."

The friends went their separate ways from the parking lot of Halstead Street Barbeque. Jix inhaled that nose-tingling, smoky balm that curls from a wood-burning fire. A canopy of stars hung overhead. Congregating patches of clouds rumored of rain by morning.

Waldo turned left toward Eva's; Jix turned right toward home. Bill's headlights in the rear-view mirror were like loving arms around her as she sped through the darkness.

Chapter Sixteen

Barefoot, pajama-clad Carol greeted her parents and immediately reported the Cochrans had finished and were pleased with the outcome. Dinah was asleep and Margee had called to say she was on her way home from play practice.

"Golly, what a day!" Jix exclaimed. "I'll catch you up on everything in the morning," she told Carol. "I can't wait to shower and get in bed, and I'm anxious to see the bedroom. I have visions of soothing lilac walls...fresh, clean, new. I'm imagining a gossamer wonderland."

"I hope you like it," Carol kissed her mother on the cheek. "I was waiting up for you and Dad. I have a busy day tomorrow. I'm scheduled to call on seven patients."

"I'm going to turn in too." Bill hugged his daughter goodnight. They heard Margee pull into the driveway. She tapped the horn to announce she was home.

At the top of the stairs, Bill stepped ahead and insisted his wife close her eyes. He pushed the bedroom door wide open, reached inside, and flicked on the overhead light. When Jix was perfectly positioned, he said, "Open your eyes, sweetheart, and see your new room."

The day had drained all but a dab of perkiness from the usually spunky woman. Her gaze moved along the wall with three side-by-side windows swathed in puddling drapes, then on to the spacious lilac wall serving as a backdrop for a king-sized bed. A fixed stare stalled on the dressing table. A lilac landslide had swallowed the six-drawer dresser with a mirror she'd gotten on her fourteenth birthday.

She examined her favorite spot in the room...the corner reading nook. Newt had put the floor lamp on the wrong side of her chintz-clad chaise lounge. The shade was crooked; books were stacked on the floor instead of on the table. *This was the big reveal?*

Deflated, she reached for Bill...her soft place to land, the man she'd dreamed of, the love of her life...and buried her face in his chest.

"Oh Bill," Jix whined. "I hate it. I hate everything about it. Lilac symbolizes first love. This screams nasty divorce."

ᴧ

Abby Gayle was eager and ready to go when Jix arrived with two beautifully restored trunks securely anchored in the bed of her pickup truck. They planned to deliver the trunks, visit Rossana and Sonya, and get back to Eva's by half past one for lunch with Eva, Margee, and Waldo.

Early morning sunshine buttered the new day with freshness and vitality. The friends merrily munched on sausages sandwiched in biscuits and chased them down with hot coffee from a fast food drive thru. Jix wadded a biscuit wrapper and handed it to her sidekick. With one hand on the steering wheel and the other grasping a paper cup, she sipped, drove, and listened to Abby Gayle tell of Austin's latest escapade on the road. Long-haul truck drivers come home with tales to tell.

"So, what didn't you like about the lilac?" Abby Gayle

changed the subject.

"It isn't so much the color. The room is too large for a pastel color. Lilac is wrong for that room. I hoped it would look better in the light of day. It looked worse."

"So, repaint it. What color is next?"

"Bill wants royal blue."

"May be too dark. No use jumping from the frying pan into the fire. Maybe a shade lighter than royal?"

"That's what I'm thinking."

"If we have time, let's stop in the paint store and look at samples," Abby Gayle suggested.

"Maybe lilac will grow on me. Newt is booked solid for a couple of months. Unless we wait, we'll have to get someone else."

"I'll ask Austin if he knows a painter. Chuck at the paint store may recommend someone. Newt Cochran is not the only painter in town."

Abby Gayle's thoughts turned to Marigold. She had called several of Marigold's friends on the chance she might discover something that had been overlooked. Crime shows on television had taught her the longer a person was missing, the less likely they would be found alive.

The conversation moved from the wrong color to the wrong neighbor. Abby Gayle had told Detective Bird and Jix of the time she'd met Lisandra Judd when the woman lived at Fairmont Manor. Memory replayed the encounter.

"I only saw her once, briefly. She was leaving Marigold's as I arrived to get Rossana. Remember when she helped me get ready for Austin's mother's visit?"

"How did Lisandra impress you?"

Abby Gayle thought for a moment. "I can't say that I was impressed. She was waiting for the elevator when I got off. She said hello, but she didn't smile...not friendly in the least. They had been arguing, but Marigold didn't discuss the matter with me. She readily dismissed it, so I thought little of it. Later, Rossana told me the woman was Lisandra Judd who lived on the eighth floor."

"We should ask Rossana if she remembers the incident. I suppose Detective Bird has talked with her this morning."

"How do you think Lisandra knew about the tunnel?" Abby Gayle asked.

"The only way she could have known is if Aaron or Marigold told her. Lisandra knew the tunnel was in the basement; she just didn't know where. Perhaps Marigold told or hinted unintentionally during a conversation about something else," Jix surmised.

"My guess would be Aaron told her. Maybe they'd dated and she discovered the grate in the closet. She lived in Fairmont Manor; they could have gotten to know each other well."

Clicking on the blinker, Jix turned into a driveway, did a highway patrol turn around, and backed to a stop at the garage door.

The trunk deliveries left happy trunk owners awed at the stunning makeovers. They expressed the ever-popular response, "This doesn't look like the same trunk."

A joyful, uplifting morning continued to improve when Jix and Abby Gayle arrived at Brookline Memorial Hospital and discovered Sonya had regained consciousness. They would visit her on the second floor and then go to the third floor to check on Rossana.

By all accounts, this had the earmarks of a good day. It would be a perfect day if they found Marigold alive and well.

Chapter Seventeen

Sonya's golden-haired, porcelain-skinned niece was ecstatic that her aunt was, as she put it, "at herself." Detective Bird had interviewed Sonya and then ordered that visitors must be approved. Jix and Abby Gayle added their names to a list, the policewoman on duty gave them the go-ahead, and they went with Klara, the niece, to Sonya's bedside.

A bandaged head and dark patches underneath her blue eyes did not dim the excitement and happiness radiating in Sonya's smile. The friends embraced, laughed, and offered thanksgiving for a favorable prognosis.

Concern for her longtime employer launched Sonya into a recount of Wednesday's horrific events.

"Today is Friday, right?" She called on Klara to clarify her time lapse.

"It was the morning of the bridge club meeting." Sonya paused to sort the correct sequence of events. "We heard the elevator while we were getting ready. You know that light that comes on above the main entrance door when the elevator stops on our floor?" They nodded. "Well, not only does it come on, but we can hear the door opening. It echoes through the foyer, so we always know when someone arrives."

She fidgeted with the bed sheet as she talked. "We didn't think much of it when the light came on. Juliet Pratt had called to say she was making flower arrangements for the tables and would bring them as soon as she finished." Sonya folded her hands and closed her eyes.

Jix patted the weary woman's shoulder. "If this is too much for you, we can come back later. Don't overextend yourself."

"No. No. We have to find Miss Marigold. I want to tell you what I told that Mrs. Bird lady."

She recalled how Lisandra Judd had caught them off guard when she burst into the apartment with a stiletto and threatened Marigold. She tearfully told how the enraged intruder flipped over the game tables, threw things, and cleared tabletops and shelves with the blade.

"She grabbed Galapago and slung him so fast I didn't have time to duck. We were so surprised; none of us knew what to do. Missy tried to calm the woman, but she had that sharp knife, and she was screaming, and it all happened so quickly." Swelling emotions cascaded over a dam of self-control.

Klara offered a box of tissues. Sonya wadded a few and mopped her eyes. When she'd regained composure, she massaged her temples with her fingers in an effort to ease a splitting headache.

The onlookers shed no tears but wept silently. Their hearts ached for this gentle woman.

"The next thing I remember, Miss Eva was trying to help me. We have to find Miss Marigold." She grabbed Jix's hand and squeezed it. "This Judd woman, she is dangerous...she's... she's a maniac!"

Jix patted her hand and vowed to find Marigold and to bring Lisandra Judd to account for her madness.

Abby Gayle gave Sonya a moment before she asked, "What

was the dispute about? Why was this woman so upset?"

Sonja told of previous encounters with the neighbor who accused Marigold of dating her male friend whom she claimed was off limits to other women. Marigold dismissed the angry woman's accusations as being absurd and outrageous, never seriously considering her capable of violence.

The visit ended abruptly when a nurse asked everyone to wait outside. After tender reassurances they would find Marigold, they bade Klara and her aunt good-bye and were off to visit Rossana.

Chapter Eighteen

A tiny television balanced on a wall bracket near the ceiling flickered, failing to capture the attention of the viewer who could not break away from mental reruns of all that had happened.

"Rossana," Jix knelt down beside her. "How are you?" She lifted a frail, limp hand draped on the arm of the chair and stroked it.

Her reply was that she was fine, but it was evident that Rossana was far from being *fine*.

When asked where Marie was, Rossana told that her sister had gone to lunch with Officer Steve Solder. She joyfully added they'd promised to bring French fries for her.

Jix and Abby Gayle were excited to hear that Rossana hoped to be discharged the following day. She was relieved when told Waldo was staying at Marigold's.

"It will be good to see Mr. Waldo, and it will be good to get home," she said. "Maybe I can wake up from this nightmare!"

They pulled chairs nearby; Jix muted the television looming overhead. Abby Gayle had baked cookies for both Rossana and Sonya. She and Jix shared a cookie as Rossana picked up her story where she'd left off the previous night.

"That crazy woman did all the talking. Missy tried to reason with her, but she wouldn't listen." Rossana leaned forward and lowered her voice to not be overheard. "I think this woman is on something…you know, like drugs or something. It is not for me to say, but she was out of control. I'm telling you; she was a wild woman!"

She leaned back and resumed her story. "I've never seen such a long, thin knife as the one she carried. It wasn't a big knife, just long. It had a sharp, tapered point." Rossana made a teepee with her fingers.

"It's called a stiletto," Abby Gayle said.

Rossana either ignored or didn't hear the comment. She splayed her fingers and waved jazz hands. "This wild woman said Miss Marigold had better leave a man named Clancy Diggs alone. When Missy tried to tell her she didn't want this man— she didn't even like this man—that she has Mr. Waldo, Lisandra Judd laughed and started throwing things. I'm telling you; she was out of control! That's when Sonya was struck in the head. I went to help my friend, but the Judd woman grabbed me and twisted my arm behind my back. She told Miss Marigold to go to the elevator and push the button to the basement or she would kill me. This mad woman said Aaron was waiting for us. You know Aaron Williams," she stated rhetorically.

Jix and Abby Gayle exchanged quick glances. Jix asked, "Why the basement? And what happened to you? We found the playing cards. Did you leave them?"

Rossana repeated Sonya's account of how Lisandra had burst into the apartment. She recalled that she had stuck cards in her pocket when distracted from setting up the game tables. Once in the basement, Marigold and the intruder scuffled, giving Rossana an opportunity to break away. Rossana was unsure of what Lisandra was looking for or why Marigold wouldn't tell her where it was located.

"She pushed Missy, and I ran to hide, but I must have fallen or fainted." She shrugged her shoulders and lifted open palms. "Everything is blank after I ran." Tears trickled down her cheeks.

"So, you didn't see them go down the tunnel?"

"Tunnel? What tunnel? We were in the basement. There is no tunnel," she exclaimed.

Abby Gayle answered, "Don't worry, Rossana. We'll tell you all about it later, or better yet, Marigold can tell you about the tunnel when we find her."

Jix hoped her friend wasn't making promises she couldn't keep.

"How were you able to squeeze into the storage area and get behind the mattress? You are petite, but even so, it would have been tricky to get inside the fencing and to move the mattress."

The puzzled woman's eyes widened. Confused and bewildered, she exclaimed, "What are you talking about? I ran. Maybe the cards fell out of my pocket. Where is this mattress?" Rossana sprung to her feet, sending the tissue box sailing.

Jix guided her to the bed and helped her get settled. Abby Gayle rang for the nurse and tried to calm the distraught woman by encouraging her to rest until they talked again.

On their way out each expressed concern that Rossana could be released from the hospital too soon. They agreed it was good that Waldo would be at Marigold's to help out.

Chapter Nineteen

"What is that divine aroma?"

Jix and Abby Gayle sniffed a trail of ginger, shallots, garlic, and sesame oil through the foyer and into the apartment.

"Are we having Chinese?" Abby Gayle was excited. Chinese food was her favorite.

Margee greeted her daughter with a hug and broke the good news that Waldo had arranged for their lunch to be catered by The Golden Canal, a local, renowned Chinese restaurant.

Jix's words streamed over her shoulder, "If he had called me, we could have gone through the drive-thru and picked up take out."

Eva joined the newcomers. "I think he wanted to do something nice for us. Mr. Allicott is putting on a good face, but he is more worried than he wants us to know. Waldo talked with a friend in Chicago who is a detective—private investigator, I think. This man isn't available to help, but he offered a few suggestions. Waldo will tell us when he gets here."

Abby Gayle was surprised. "Where is Waldo?" She pulled back her sleeve to see her wristwatch as she sat down next to Jix on a sofa that resembled an upholstered surfboard with spindly legs and a bolstered back.

"He called to say he is running late and we should go ahead and eat. He asked that we save him egg noodles in peanut sauce or cashew chicken or both." Margee laughed.

A woman with jet-black hair, wearing a traditional Cheongsam dress and cotton Mary Jane's, came from the kitchen carrying a pot of jasmine tea and four cups on a bamboo tray. She cordially greeted the ladies and asked if she should serve or if they preferred to. Margee volunteered and poured everyone a cup of subtly sweet, fragrant tea. A profusion of jasmine blossoms scented the room like fairy dust.

"Ah," Eva savored the soothing brew. "I'd like to drink till my heart's content and then take a bath in jasmine tea."

Jix chuckled. "Sounds wonderful." Steering the conversation into troubled waters, she asked her mother, "Mom, did you find out what Bryson is up to?"

Margee set her cup on the mirrored coffee table. An exasperated sigh preceded a tale of her visit with lawyer Pennington. "Charles met with me and two other members of the Board of Trustees. To cut to the chase, let me state that how the Foundation is managed is a joke and an insult to our intelligence. No one oversees daily activities even though several self-appointed administrators or officers think they are in charge. They bicker and contradict one another, and nothing gets done. The result is a lot of thunder but not much rain."

"I guess everyone just assumes that Marigold is running things," Eva poured another cup of tea.

"Apparently, she isn't. No one is. Marigold is so set in her ways she can be a bit intimidating; therefore, she doesn't always work well with others. I can't deny that. Regardless of the source of disorder, whatever or whoever that may be, a chain of command is nonexistent," Margee replied. "The Board meets annually, and a special meeting can be called anytime as needed.

If a meeting isn't requested, we assume things are running smoothly. Bryson has gained far too much power. And I'm not certain who is aware of the liberties he has either been given or taken on himself. Charles is probing into the details. It is indeed possible that Bryson has sabotaged us. I hope not."

Abby Gayle reasoned, "Because his grandfather has been active from the start, it stands to reason others would trust Mr. Purefoy to oversee how business is conducted and do what is best for the good of the Foundation."

"In a perfect world, dear. Clifford isn't young anymore, and he isn't as sharp as he once was…and that is putting it kindly. Charles has called a meeting of the Board and all officers to be held at three tomorrow afternoon. He's summoned Clifford and Bryson to attend. We'll confront the Purefoys and see what they have to say."

A server came to announce lunch was ready.

"We need to be at that meeting; if it is open to interested parties," Abby Gayle said to Eva. They took a seat at the dining room table.

"We all need to attend," said Jix. "And I have to work on trunks tomorrow no matter who does what. By the way, Eva, there are five trunks in the basement. Do they belong to anyone? Are they for sale?"

Eva scooted her chair closer to the table. "They've been stored there for as long as I've been superintendent. I have no idea who they belong to. They can belong to you if you want them. No charge."

The table was loaded with bowls and plates of rice, sweet and sour chicken, lemon chicken, Szechwan beef and broccoli, and egg drop soup… to name a few.

Margee lamented, "It's a shame to start without Waldo. I wonder what's keeping him. It is unlike him to not call when he is running late."

Jix spooned from a bowl of something drowned in hot-pink

sauce. "Eva, I'd like to restore one of the little trunks as my gift to you?"

Eva bit into a spring roll and closed her eyes to savor the deliciousness. Before taking another scrumptious bite, she uttered, "Oh my! That would be delightful!"

As the midday meal wound down, questions as to Waldo's whereabouts turned from curiosity into grave concern. The servers cleared the table and placed a fortune cookie before each of the ladies.

"Oh, goodie!" Eva's eyes sparkled with anticipation. "This is the best part of a Chinese meal." She cracked the cookie and pulled a strip of paper from inside. Everyone listened. "An acquaintance from the past will affect you in the future."

Abby Gayle declared the prediction fulfilled. "That hit the nail on the head. Lisandra from the past has affected the future. Let's see what profound prediction awaits me." She broke open the cookie.

Unfurling the tiny slip of paper with her fingers, Abby Gayle read, "A dubious friend may be an enemy in camouflage." All agreed the fortunes were spot on.

"This is very strange," Abby Gayle said as Jix snapped her fortune cookie in half.

Everyone was on edge as Jix pulled the sliver of paper from the broken wafer. She read to herself before reading aloud.

"An inch of time is an inch of gold." She looked to the others for comments. "Whatever does that mean?" Jix folded the fortune and tucked it in her shirt pocket.

Margee quipped, "It means nothing, as do the other fortunes. I've never known a fortune cookie that could be trusted."

Before Margee could read her fortune, an obviously distraught Waldo rushed into the room carrying a newspaper.

"Waldo!" Margee exclaimed. "We were worried something had happened to you."

He tossed the newspaper onto the table and declared, "We

have plenty to worry about! Read this!"

Margee patted the chair next to her. "Come, sit down, Waldo. Calm down; tell us where you've been."

He remained standing. "I can't sit down. Marigold is in greater danger than we ever imagined."

Everyone scrambled to read the headline. "What does this mean? Who are these people?" Abby Gayle picked up the paper and read the first paragraph aloud then handed it to Jix.

"I wouldn't have known who they are had I not called on Clancy Diggs." Waldo talked faster and louder than necessary. "He told me these are two women Lisandra Judd shared a condo with after leaving Fairmont Manor. I went from his place to report this to Detective Bird. We have plenty to worry about. The situation is worse than we imagined. Marigold has been kidnapped by a woman who stabbed both her roommates on Wednesday morning and left them for dead!"

A tinge of fear quickened her heart. Margee stared at the headlines unwilling to accept that the person responsible for the stabbings now held Marigold against her will.

"But we don't know that Lisandra Judd did this," she said.

Waldo was short on patience. "Margee, her involvement is not difficult to see. I know it is difficult to accept, but it is what it is. Marigold is being held captive by a dangerous, violent, out-of-control individual who is obviously capable of murder."

Jix spoke on her mother's behalf, "Waldo, everyone is aware of the extreme seriousness of the situation. There is nothing to be gained by being curt."

Abby Gayle supported Jix. "We have to hope this happened in a fit of anger and things are calmer now. And we mustn't underestimate how clever and bold Marigold can be. Let's focus on positive possibilities, slim as they may be."

Waldo plopped down in a chair. "Of course. Forgive me. This has been a blow to the gut." He rubbed the back of his neck. "Marigold and I have been steady friends for the last few years. I don't think I've ever once told her I love her. I've told her that I care for her, and she is special to me. I do so wish I had told her that I truly love her."

Jix patted his shoulder. "You can tell her as soon as she gets home."

Margee looked down at the tiny cookie fortune she clutched with her fingers. Before she wadded it and tossed it in her cup of tea, she read, *the strong person understands how to withstand a substantial loss.*

Cookie fortunes were for the superstitious. Margee Fairmont was not superstitiously inclined.

Chapter Twenty

"So, let me get this straight." Shirtless, Bill Haynes peddled a stationary bicycle effortlessly. "Bryson has pirated the Foundation?"

"I don't know what he's done. Mother hopes to find out more tomorrow." Jix sat on the chaise lounge with an opened book on her outstretched legs. "By all accounts, he's taken control, but no one knows if or how, just yet. He may have filed for dissolution of the Foundation and sought to dispose of its primary asset, Fairmont Manor."

Bill dismissed the likelihood. "I don't see how he could manage a takeover or how he could file for dissolution. That has to be a complicated process. If he has conducted a dissolution and transfer of assets without signatures from members of the Board of Trustees, he is one smart cookie…so smart, he deserves to enjoy the spoils of his quest."

"Or he is incredibly stupid and has made a mess for someone to clean up."

"Well, that too," Bill agreed.

Jix put the book on a table, slung her feet to the floor and stood. "I wouldn't go as far as to congratulate him. And if he has pirated the property, that leaves Marigold and the tenants without a home."

She opened the closet door and took her nightgown off a hook.

"Once it is revealed to what lengths he has gone, there will be a legal battle to undo his dastardly deeds, assuming they can be undone," she said as she disappeared into the bathroom.

"Dastardly deeds, he-he," Bill chuckled at a mental image of Dick Dastardly, his favorite animated character on Saturday morning cartoons. "Turn on the shower, please," he shouted as he cut his exercise routine short and plopped down on the bed to take off his shoes.

Jix tuned the water flow and temperature to just right and passed her husband as he stepped into the shower. She sat down at her dressing table, intentionally avoiding looking at the lilac walls.

She called loud enough through the open door so he could hear over spray from the showerhead, "Go by the paint store tomorrow, and pick up the new paint. Chuck has set aside five gallons, but if you don't like it, get whatever color you want." She brushed her hair and waited for him to answer.

"I will. Waldo knows a fellow that paints. He's coming tomorrow to give an estimate. Fellow named Theo Somebody."

"I'll be gone. Mother will be here."

He shut off the water and threw a towel over his dripping hair.

"Where are you going?" Clothed in a towel wrap, he retrieved a comb from his pants pocket to slick his sopping brown hair in place. "I can't find my comb. The one I leave in the vanity drawer is gone."

"I'll look for it," she said. "Get dressed and come sit down. I want to tell you something."

Bill tied the string to his pajama pants and took a seat on the chaise lounge. "What?"

"I talked with Avonelle Bird this afternoon. She hasn't put out an all points bulletin for Marigold's car because of several leads as to where they may have gone. Waldo talked to the man who is at the center of the dispute, and he suggested three places Lisandra Judd may have taken Marigold and Aaron."

"Who is this man?"

"Someone named Clancy Diggs."

Bill jumped up, threw his hands in the air, and shouted, "Please tell me you are kidding! You can't be serious!"

Taken by surprise, Jix asked, "You know him?"

"Suffice it to say, I know him. Nothing he says is reliable. If he told Waldo where to look, he is very likely sending him on a wild goose chase. Clancy is like a deranged arsonist who is a front-row spectator at fires he starts."

"Tell Waldo these things."

"Honey, why can't we just leave matters like this to law enforcement?" He pleaded. "They are trained to capture criminals. They get paid. This is their job."

She put the top on a jar of cold cream. "My concern is for Marigold and Aaron. What would we do without Marigold Fairmont? I want Dinah to grow up with Marigold in her life. Remember the first time Dinah called her Goldie? We were amused and amazed. I want Dinah's Goldie in our lives for as long as possible." Tears stung her eyes.

Bill pulled her into his arms. "I do too, sweetheart, but why would Clancy Diggs think he knows where they may be?"

He held her close and stroked her hair.

"Apparently, he knows Lisandra, and he knew the two women who were her roommates. All three were fighting over him."

"I'm sure they were," Bill commented with a touch of asperity in his tone. "He's such a prized catch."

She kissed him and then sat down on her side of the bed.

Easing under the cover, she stretched out and wiggled into a restful position. "He knows of a quarry where Lisandra has friends that may have provided another vehicle or helped her in some way. Waldo says Clancy also suggested a cabin just over the state line in the National Forest."

"Are the police aware of this?"

"I don't know. When I talked to Detective Bird, she said they are following every lead. Whether Clancy's leads are included, I can't say."

Bill climbed into bed and flicked off the bedside lamp. When darkness filled the room, Jix commented, "Thank goodness, the lilac is gone."

"It isn't gone."

"At least I can't see it."

"Has anyone called her car phone?"

Chapter Twenty-One

Bright morning sun streamed through the windshield of Abby Gayle's newly acquired Cadillac. She'd bragged to Jix that the car wasn't a current model (nineteen eighty-nine), but it had low mileage and handled like a dream.

"It's beautiful, and it also rides like floating on a cloud." The blue leather passenger seat was as comfortable as Jix's recliner at home.

A brief stop for breakfast at Delores' Diner before heading out of town, then down the highway to Barrow's Crossing where they turned off the main road and began a long, winding climb up Sander's Mountain. Brisk early October air signaled to the trees to shed summer green and put on shades of magenta, crimson, and gold.

The blacktop soon ended, and the Caddy bounced onto a gravel and dirt road that stretched to the crest of the mountain. Abby Gayle drove slowly to create less dust and to avoid ruts and potholes.

"So, no one answered the car phone," Abby Gayle repeated what Jix had told her.

"No. We called last night and several times this morning. Bill asked the operator to verify the number and that the phone is working.

"Look!" She waved out the window to a couple in a canoe gliding down the creek snaking alongside the roadway. The two stopped paddling and returned an exuberant greeting. "Let's go canoeing before it gets too cold."

Abby Gayle glanced past her passenger and tooted the horn. "Could do. They rent canoes at Pearson's Pond." They continued in the opposite direction of the canoers. "Back to the car phone. Either Marigold hasn't had an opportunity to call or she is afraid to."

"Or both. Or there isn't service wherever they are. Bill knows about mobile unit frequencies and requirements. I only know two people who have, or can afford, a car phone…Marigold and Waldo."

"And the quarry…how did you get this information?"

"Clancy Diggs told Waldo, who is on his way to a wilderness area across the state line while we are checking out the rock quarry which isn't far, about a quarter of the way to the crest." Jix took off her jacket. "Time to peel the first layer," she said, to rising temperatures.

"Why a rock quarry?" Abby Gayle slowed and moved to the edge of the road as a loaded dump truck approached. "I hope he doesn't sling gravel on my car."

"Lisandra has friends who either own the quarry or work there. My information is second hand; Clancy told Waldo, who told me. We'll have to feel our way around, and we may find nothing. Bill says Clancy isn't trustworthy."

Once the truck and a cloud of dust had passed, Abby Gayle braked to a stop and shifted the gear into park. She stepped out of the car and unzipped her jacket. It was the time of year with cool nights and toasty daytime temperatures. She inhaled deeply. The woodsy mountain air was as refreshing as a drink of cool water on a sweltering day.

A symphony of birdsong drifted in the open window. Nature spread peace and contentment like frosting a cake. If only Jix could find her mother's cousin and bring her home to safety, it would be a perfect day.

They resumed their trek to the quarry, watching for signage indicating where to turn. A sign cautioning that trucks were entering the roadway guaranteed they were close.

"Stonewall Quarry." Jix pointed to a weathered sign indicating they should turn left.

The Cadillac crept along a rutted, washed out entrance. Abby Gayle pulled onto roadside brush to dodge the ruts.

"We should have brought the truck," Jix said. "Earl is picking up the trunks from Eva today, or I would have driven."

Abby Gayle kept her eyes on the task at hand. "One day of roadwork and they will have repaired damage left by recent rains. We're fine in the car, but you owe me a carwash."

"Duly noted. That white trailer ahead must be the office. Let's park here and walk in."

"We are entering a hard hat area."

"A hard head will have to do for now," Jix joked, as the Caddy rolled to a stop underneath the only tree in sight.

"You got a plan, Sherlock?" Abby Gayle asked, as they approached the trailer with a sign propped in a window identifying it as the office.

"Something will come to me."

They climbed a set of black, wrought iron steps to a small porch and opened the door.

"Hello," Jix called to an empty room.

A woman emerged from the back and took a seat at a desk with a name plaque. Presumably, the middle-age woman with big hair was *Blanche Meyers, Office Manager*. She greeted the ladies and asked how she might be of help.

Smiling sweetly, Jix told of an upcoming field trip for her

fifth-grade students. She and her vice-principal, Miss Wiggins, had come for information on quarry tours and also to assess safety issues for school children.

The secretary wearing jelly shoes and a blouse with overstuffed shoulder pads assured the visitors that tours were perfectly safe. Inviting the ladies to make themselves at home, she left to fetch someone named Colton, who was filling in temporarily as tour guide.

"Miss Wiggins? I'm Miss Wiggins? You've watched too many Carol Burnett shows."

Jix burst out laughing. "You are the perfect Miss Wiggins. Woo Colton into telling us if they know Lisandra."

Abby Gayle broke into laughter. The last thing she wanted to do was to woo Colton, but when Colton held the door open for Blanche, and they stepped inside, it was plain to see that would not be an unpleasant task.

The tall, handsome, young man with sky blue eyes offered a mini tour of the grounds. He plucked two yellow, hard hats off a shelf and ushered the ladies out the door. He didn't say so, but his actions indicated he was a busy man, and this would be a brief excursion.

Chapter Twenty-Two

A beehive of noise and activity, bobbing yellow hard hats added contrast to an open pit of prismatic blocks of stone. Heavy machinery roared and spewed plumes of diesel exhaust fumes like fire-breathing dragons. Dump trucks, conditioned for impact, waited as patiently as pack mules for loaders to pile fifty tons of rock in their beds. Crushed stone rattled on conveyor belts where the stones were sized and then stockpiled.

Colton pointed out a gigantic machine used to scrape loose rock from the walls of the pit to maintain safety. He demonstrated with hand gestures how holes were bored to plant dynamite to blast sections of the stone wall.

"This is amazing," Jix said. She and Abby Gayle observed from a wooden platform fifteen feet off the ground.

"How often do you blast?" Abby Gayle asked. She could envision a car blown into a zillion pieces so it or anyone inside could never be identified. Had Lisandra envisioned the same?

"Depends...once a month...once a week."

Massive machines pushed and loaded tons of dirt and stone as easily as Jix swept her kitchen floor—perhaps as easily as burying a car so deep it would never be found. She reigned in her imagination and asked, "Colton, who owns this quarry?"

"Clancy Diggs. Local fellow. We don't see much of him. He isn't involved in daily operations."

The women exchanged questioning looks. Why would Clancy Diggs tell Waldo to check the quarry and not reveal that he was the owner?

They walked back to the office and stood outside near the entrance. Colton was anxious to get back to work and did not linger after they'd said their goodbyes. As he turned to leave, Abby Gayle seized their last chance for information. She hailed him to ask one more question. "Do you know Lisandra Judd?"

Colton stopped in his tracks, turned, and retraced his steps, "What school do you teach at?"

Jix ignored the question. "We are looking for Lisandra Judd. Clancy Diggs suggested that someone here may have seen her recently, or know where she may be. If he owns the place, he could have asked."

"And you couldn't just say that? You have taken my time when you have no intention of setting up a tour. Lady, you have some nerve! I have a dozen things going on. I'm needed in ten places. While we stand here socializing, things are not being done because I am not there to supervise. And yet, I've spent valuable time with you like we're at a Sunday afternoon picnic in the park. Where do you come off thinking you have the right to do that?"

"You're right, and I apologize. Please forgive me, but if we'd shown up and started asking questions, would you have been forthcoming with answers? To be truly honest, Colton, I'm desperate. I'm grabbing at straws. Our cousin and her companion are missing. Lisandra Judd has taken them against their wills. Everything we hear indicates she is dangerous, and hope for their safe return is slipping away." Tears welled in Jix's eyes. "They've been missing several days."

Colton's anger melted as quickly as it had flared. He looked into the clouds overhead, then he looped his thumbs in his pants pockets and looked at the ground. "Lisandra is Clancy's girlfriend…of sorts; he has more than one girlfriend. I haven't seen Lisandra recently, but I'll ask around." He uttered a warning, "You need to be careful. Be very careful. Give me your phone number, and I'll give you a call if I can find out anything."

Jix reached in her jeans' pocket and pulled out her wallet. She located and presented Colton with one of her brand new *Trunk Doctor* business cards. "Just got new cards," she said. "You're the first to get one." If he was impressed, it didn't show.

Abby Gayle thanked him for the tour and expressed how much she'd enjoyed it, again apologizing for any inconvenience.

Colton mumbled sarcastically that he had loved every minute of it and walked away.

"Let's look at the trunks." Jix spotted three trunks on the ground near the truck where Earl had left them.

Abby Gayle inched the Cadillac up the Haynes' driveway and parked behind Margee's car. "I can't stay long." She checked the dashboard clock. "I need to go home and do a few things before we meet at three to hear what the Purefoys have to say. I'll take a quick peek at the trunks, and then off I go."

Earl came outside when he heard the car doors slammed. "Hey! We got some beauties here. I dropped off the two small ones that are locked at Ernie Lawson's." The third generation locksmith ran Lawson's Locksmith and Bicycle Repair Shop.

"Thanks, Earl. I'll stop by after we attend a meeting and see if he has opened them."

"And…" Earl said, "…a painter named Theo came by about the bedroom. I sent him inside to talk to your mother."

"Thanks. I'll check with her."

Abby Gayle stacked yellowed, smelly books.

"Nothing worth saving here." Jix opened a book and a silver fish scurried from the pages. "Earl, please close these books in the metal can behind the shop. The last thing we need around here is an infestation of silver fish."

"You may as well throw away these baby clothes." Abby Gayle held up a moldy baby shirt. They salvaged picture frames and stacked them against a workbench. Three old paint-by-number paintings were designated as donations to the thrift store.

Jix lifted the lid on the large camel back trunk. The hinge needed to be replaced to prop the lid open. She pulled one of six cardboard tubes from inside and then closed the heavy lid.

"We looked in these when we first found the trunks. It's wallpaper." Jix twisted the cap off and pulled out a roll. Once unrolled on the tailgate of the truck, the three were surprised at the mint condition of the obviously expensive paper.

"This is the same paper that is in Marigold's bedroom. It is beautiful, so unique. Look how the gold shines in sunlight. It almost looks real."

Crystal lake blue with a night sky undertone peeped through a brilliant gold pattern of roses. "Remember, Abby Gayle? The papered rooms match nothing else in her apartment. She has Art Deco throughout except her bedroom and a sitting room... and I think the hallway."

"Didn't she say her father had it custom made and when she redecorated in Art Deco, for sentimental reasons, she didn't change anything in the bedroom? He loved the papered walls and he had said he never wanted to replace this pattern."

"Yes, she did. I'll take these back to Marigold. I doubt she even knows there are spare rolls."

She rewound the heavy, velvety paper and slid it back in the tube. As instructed, Earl took all six rolls to the office where he stacked them in the closet.

Abby Gayle turned to leave. "I'm off like a pair of old bloomers." She waved and headed for her car.

"See you at Charles Pennington's office at three."

Jix waved as her friend backed down the long, steep driveway. Pulled in half a dozen directions, she looked at the trunks stacked against the garage vying for her attention. Not only did she need to work on trunks, it was time to see about lunch. And then there was the ever-looming, disastrous bedroom that had to be de-lilaced.

There wasn't much time until she would be off to the lawyer's office. Soon Dora Keeling, long-time friend and next-door neighbor, would come to stay with Dinah while Foundation members confronted Clifford and Bryson Purefoy.

Jix's heart won over practical reasoning. She was going inside to get Dinah, and they were going to the sand box in the backyard and make frog houses. Everything else would wait, but Dinah was growing up, and building frog houses is for little children and their grandmas.

Dinah loved for Jix to firmly pack damp sand over her tiny, bare toes, then carefully slide her foot out while she cautioned the toddler not to wiggle her little piggies and cause a cave in. They would leave a sand box filled with sand igloos the size of Dinah's foot—houses fit for the finest frog families.

Chapter Twenty-Three

Lawyer Pennington called the meeting to order. He had done his homework. Listeners were shocked when financial reports exposed the Purefoy's unauthorized activities. Documentation of correspondence with the state's Attorney General spelled out how Bryson had misused his post as financial director. He had given himself a position of substantial influence as well as using his grandfather's place in the Foundation's hierarchy to further his cause. Clifford Purefoy's signature was on much of the paperwork, but it was soon apparent that he had signed anything his grandson had asked him to, perhaps unaware of Bryson's goals—perhaps not.

Chairman of the Board, John Weaver, gave Bryson an opportunity to present exculpatory evidence. Bryson offered no defense. He replied with an air of arrogance, "Everything is legal and within my realm of authority. Fairmont Foundation is in the process of being dissolved and its assets transferred. I'll take possession of Fairmont Manor immediately."

And without further ado, the feathers hit the fan. Everyone began talking and screaming at once.

Confused and upset, Clifford Purefoy was ushered from the proceedings and taken to his home. Bryson's attorney, Charles Cyrix, defended his client's actions and shouted over the others that he would see the lot of them in court. He grabbed his brief case and his client and left a room filled with frustrated, angry, betrayed men and women.

Angry as a swatted wasp, Jix threw her truck keys on the kitchen countertop. She and her mother had tried to find something positive about the mess Bryson Purefoy had created. The part where the entire episode could have been avoided if the foundation had been properly monitored was difficult to swallow.

"Dinah's asleep," shushed Dora Keeling. The jovial friend gathered her belongings and stepped toward the door. "Sorry to rush, but if I hurry, I can get to the bank before it closes. Everything went well. Carol called to check on Dinah and to say she would be an hour or so late getting home."

Margee walked with Dora outside and expressed many thanks for babysitting. She waved goodbye and watched her neighbor make her way across the lawn. No sooner had she stepped back inside than Dora's smiling face popped up at the door again.

"Oh, Jix. A man called for you several times. He wouldn't leave a message but said it is urgent. His number is on the telephone pad. Bye again." She eased the screen door shut.

Abby Gayle had followed Jix from the meeting in her car. She sat down at the table while Margee poured iced tea and set out the remains of a coconut cream pie. "We'll have to pretend we're at a pie tasting…there's not much left."

"I'll get plates." Abby Gayle got up to fetch dessert plates and cut the quarter of a pie into three slim slices.

Jix read Dora's note and with wide-eyed excitement shared

that Colton had called. "He says to return his call as soon as possible. He has vital information."

"Well, get to calling," Margee instructed.

As she dialed the number, Jix asked if someone would make coffee. Abby Gayle made short order of the request and sat back down to hear a one-sided conversation with the reluctant tour guide.

Jix mouthed to the ladies that he had answered.

"Hello. Colton, this is Jix Haynes returning your call."

"Really. Let me jot this down." She ripped off the top page of the pad with Dora's note on it and poised to write on the blank page.

It was quiet enough to hear a butterfly pass gas.

Jix listened to Colton. Abby Gayle and Margee listened to her.

"I see. Do you think this is reliable information?" More listening.

Jix scribbled on the lined page.

"Uh-huh. Uh-huh. How far is it from here?" Pause. "I see. You think six or seven hours?"

The ladies at the table were motionless as they hung onto every word.

"It will be worth looking into. Thank you so much, Colton. I appreciate you taking time to call. Just one more thing…what can you tell me about Mr. Diggs? I haven't met him, and I've heard mixed reviews."

The quarry foreman talked on. Jix listened intently, now and then injecting an uh-huh.

"I'll make plans to check this out. Thank you. Thanks, Colton. May I call you if I need more information? Thanks so much."

She rotely replaced the telephone receiver. A shake of her head did little to clear it; a moment was required to process Colton's overwhelming news.

Grasping the notes she'd taken, she reported, "Colton says he knows where Lisandra has taken Marigold and Aaron."

Chapter Twenty-Four

"She's alive. Oh, Hallelujah!" Margee clapped her hands and bounced in the chair. "Where did he say they are?"

Abby Gayle spoke first. "Come and sit down." She pulled the chair next to her away from the table. Jix slid onto it.

"On an island in the Gulf of Mexico. Mother, is the coffee ready?"

Margee scooted her chair away from the table and patted her daughter on the shoulder as she darted past. "It is."

"Start at the beginning and tell us everything he said," Abby Gayle reached for the note pad.

Jix repeated the gist of the conversation. Colton had met Clancy Diggs earlier that day for lunch on the premise of discussing business at the quarry. After lunch and a few drinks, the conversation had turned to Lisandra. Colton mentioned to Clancy that someone had come to the quarry looking for her. When asked if he had heard from his girlfriend, Clancy admitted they'd talked that morning.

Colton told Jix that Lisandra was staying in Clancy's beach house on a small island off the coast. He knew the location from having been there when he'd won a trip for an exceptional safety record at the quarry. He also cautioned that Clancy could be lying.

Margee set coffee beside Jix's uneaten sliver of pie. "Call Detective Bird. They'll either send law enforcement from that area or go themselves."

"Supposedly Lisandra threatened to kill them and herself if Clancy contacts the police."

Sorting relief, uncertainty, and indecisiveness, the three women silently pondered the situation and their next move.

Abby Gayle voiced her opinion. "It makes no sense to act on second-hand information. It's too far to go, and the risks are too great based on what Colton says Clancy Diggs said. Everybody and his brother must be looking for Lisandra. The stabbings are all over the newspapers. The police know she assaulted Sonya and kidnapped Marigold and Aaron."

"Then all we have to do is continue to wait," Margee said. "The police will find them."

"There's something about this whole thing that is puzzling... there's something we don't know that we need to know." Jix drummed her fingers on the table. "I keep going back to Clancy Diggs. If Clancy knows where Lisandra is, in spite of her threats, he should be compelled to call Detective Bird. Any way you look at it, lives are at risk. What is he hiding? Why does he not want to get involved?"

Abby Gayle added, "Even if she threatened to harm the others and herself, why wouldn't Diggs do something. An anonymous tip...anything. If he knows where they are, he could get that information to the police without getting directly involved. Why wouldn't he want them to be located?"

"Well, we would do something to help find them because that's who we are," said Margee, "but we don't know Clancy Diggs. We don't know anything about him. For instance, what else, if anything, is he a part of other than owning a quarry?"

"Colton says he owns several businesses in the county. Diggs is his boss, so Colton may be reluctant to express his true opinion about the man," Jix answered.

"Waldo went to the cabin in the forest, and he found no more than you did when you went to the quarry," Margee reminded them. "It makes no sense that he sent you to a quarry he owns to find people he said were there that were not. If he had truly been looking for Lisandra, he would have simply called the quarry and asked if or when anyone had seen her."

Jix said, "Bill, as usual, is right. Diggs trustworthiness is questionable."

"You think?" was the sarcastic response.

"And Abby Gayle's right. We can't risk wasting more time. For all we know, Lisandra may have disposed of Marigold and Aaron, and Clancy Diggs is playing us to allow time for her to get away."

"Oh!" Margee gasped and slapped her hand over her heart.

"Sorry, Mother. I'm just speculating. I'm hopeful that Marigold has found a way to pacify Lisandra and keep everyone safe until we can locate them."

"Back to the crux of the matter," Abby Gayle had eaten her sampling of pie between comments and was eyeing Margee's. "We should eliminate the possibility of wasting more time. We don't need to drive hours to a place we've never been until we are more certain we will find them there."

Jix wondered, "Why would Clancy tell Colton he had talked to Lisandra? What if he has gotten involved in something that blew up in his face? Maybe he doesn't know what to do. Maybe he needs someone to talk to...to help him decide what to do next."

Abby Gayle latched onto Jix with an intuitive stare. "Are you thinking what I am thinking?"

Jix nodded over the rim of her cup. She shoveled a bite of pie with her fork. "I think so."

"Well, I'm not psychic. You'll have to tell me what you two are thinking. I'm totally clueless," Margee said.

"We need to have a little chat with Clancy Diggs immediately," Jix said. Abby Gayle agreed.

"Fact of the matter is, we should have had a chat with him days ago."

Abby Gayle asked how they would find an address for the man.

"It's a little before five." She looked at the apple clock on the wall. "Where would he be this time of day?"

"I have no idea where he is, but as for an address," Margee went for the phone book, "let's look in the most logical place."

Chapter Twenty-Five

A flurry of fact-finding netted a home address and phone number for Clancy Diggs. Jix asked what Bill would do in a similar situation, and their next move was clear as a bell. Be truthful.

She dialed the number and was given another number by the housekeeper. A bystander at Billy Jack's Billiards called Diggs to the phone. Jix asked if they might meet, as she needed his help in a life and death matter. When he hesitated, she added if he weren't available, she could talk with the police. Reluctantly, he agreed to meet at one of his businesses within the hour.

Jix and Abby Gayle headed to the seedier side of downtown. Their destination: *I Digg It Supper and Social Club*.

As instructed by Diggs, the ladies knocked on the back alley door. A shapely young lady clothed in a red bustier, which had brilliantly boosted her bosoms to lofty heights, cracked the door and asked what they wanted. Once convinced that Clancy awaited their arrival, the woman with long legs wrapped in fishnet stockings, led them upstairs to a room at the end of a lengthy hallway.

There they met the infamous Mr. Diggs. The fifty- something man was scarcely taller than a Christmas elf, albeit, much better looking than the typical elf illustrated in children's books. Gold studs filled piercings in his ears; a tattoo peeped from his v-neck shirt. His shoulder-length gray hair was slicked back and neatly clasped into a ponytail. A fuzzy face suggested he had not shaved in several days.

He greeted the ladies warmly and invited them to sit down, remarking more than once that his time was limited.

Jix gazed across a cluttered desk at the little man in a big chair. His coal-black eyes darted about like a rabbit on the run; he was fidgety, perhaps troubled. Smoke curled from a cigar propped on the edge of an ashtray. Seeping from an unknown source, The Rolling Stones...turned down low...complained about not getting any satisfaction.

"Mr. Diggs." Jix had made introductions, and then taken a seat in a room with a library-look, heavily laden with smoke and stale air.

"Call me Clancy."

She smiled. "Clancy. Our time is also limited. I'll get right to the point. We have a mutual friend, Marigold Fairmont. She is not only a very good friend, but we are related through my father."

The man studied Jix's face. Then he swung his gaze toward Abby Gayle. When he didn't respond verbally, Abby Gayle asked, "Do you know Marigold Fairmont?"

He swallowed hard. "Yes. We are acquaintances." He picked up the smoldering cigar, drew on it, and slowly blew smoke before placing it in the ashtray.

His visitors held their breaths and wished for a wave of fresh air.

"Do you know Lisandra Judd?" Jix noted an immediate tenseness in his already clenched jaw. He shuffled his position in the chair and crossed his legs.

"Why do you want to know?" He answered with a question.

Jix looked down at her hands folded in her lap. While Mr. Diggs sized up her and her friend, she had looked deep into his dark eyes. The fellow was an aging hippie. *Did hippies still preach love as they had in the sixties?* she wondered.

Jix's knowledge of hippies would fit in a walnut shell, but she was desperate, and the clock was ticking. Everyone concerned for Marigold was at the end of their rope. Hopefully, Diggs was at the end of his. Bill's warning of the man lingered like a protective mother warning no, no, no with a wagging finger.

A tiny tear escaped and trickled down her cheek. She quickly brushed it away.

"Let's not play games, Clancy. Marigold is missing. For reasons unknown to us, we know Lisandra Judd has taken her and her associate. My mother is on the brink of a breakdown. We are worried sick. Marigold is not a young woman. She doesn't have medications she needs. Her employee Aaron is in poor health. If Lisandra doesn't kill them, they'll die from lack of medical care. We need to find them and end this nightmare."

Chapter Twenty-Six

"Please tell us what you know, and let's work together to avoid a tragic outcome. We may be able to prevent the death of your friend Lisandra and the others."

Jix rested her case. The ball was in Clancy's court.

Abby Gayle held her breath when the little man began to blink rapidly. Perhaps the man had a nervous tic. Was he on the brink of telling all, or he was convulsing? She said, "Help us before something irreversible happens. We will have to live knowing we could have prevented a tragic ending but did nothing to stop it," she pleaded.

Clancy bowed his head and closed his eyes. No one spoke. No one moved.

Smoke swirled from the cigar.

The Stones had sung their song, and in the background Bobbie Gentry strummed an Ode to Billie Joe.

As melodramatic as a Shakespearean actor, Diggs raised his head, stood, and moved around the desk. He pushed a pile of papers out of the way and parked his behind on the corner. With one short leg dangling, the tip of his other shoe barely touched the floor. Well-developed biceps flexed when he clasped his hands in his lap.

With a level gaze, he spun his tale.

"For the last six years, Lisandra has struggled with an addiction to morphine." He crossed his arms, and tucked trembling hands underneath his elbows.

"She was injured in a helicopter accident in 1983 when she was an army nurse on a medical team that took part in the Invasion of Grenada," he said.

"Their helicopter crashed. The bird flipped on its side, and Lisandra was seriously injured when a heavy metal gurney fell on her. Her shoulder and hip were fractured, causing unbearable pain. She was in an army hospital for four months, and during that time she became addicted to morphine. This has changed her from a sweet, lovable woman into the volatile person she has become."

His shoulders sagged. He paused as if contemplating telling more. Hesitantly, he added, "She started using heroin about a year ago."

"That explains a lot." Jix reached over and touched Abby Gayle's arm. Her friend squeezed her hand.

"Where is she, Clancy?" Abby Gayle cut to the chase.

He ignored the question. "Allow me to bring you ladies up to date on how we have arrived at the situation we now face," he said.

"Six months or so ago, Lisandra became extremely possessive of me. I was totally knocked for a loop because we had been nothing more than friends for years. Good friends. Well, perhaps on a few occasions, more than just friends, but there were never terms of commitment on my part. Lisandra wanted to marry, not I." He moved back to his chair and sat down.

While his back was turned, Jix rolled her eyes at Abby Gayle.

Elbows on the desk, fingers entwined, he continued, "I thought if she moved from Fairmont Manor into a condo with two sisters I'd been seeing off and on, Lisandra would see we were nothing more than friends. Instead, she became insanely jealous."

"These are the women Lisandra stabbed last Wednesday morning?"

"Yes. Stacy and Shaleece Shepherd. Both are recovering; it is nothing short of a miracle they survived. Lisandra flew into an all-out tirade with anyone in her path!"

Abby Gayle asked, "What was her problem with Marigold?"

"For the last eight months or so, Lisandra has been angry with everyone about everything. She is paranoid; she's delusional. Drugs have totally consumed her. From what the Shepherd sisters tell me, Lisandra thought Marigold and I were an item and therefore a threat to her."

A loud disturbance downstairs drew the attention of Diggs. He flew to the door, cracked it open, and listened for a moment.

"Sorry ladies!" He scurried around the desk to the far side of the room and stopped near floor-to-ceiling bookcases filled with colorful volumes and knick-knacks.

Abby Gayle jumped to her feet and spun around at the sound of a host of footsteps clambering up the stairs. "What's happening?"

"I don't know, but it doesn't sound good."

Thunderous footfall drummed down the lengthy corridor. Jix grabbed Abby Gayle's arm. "We should take cover or run!"

"Ask Cl…," she looked about the room.

The little man was nowhere to be seen. A hinged bookcase that concealed a hidden passageway was inches away from closing behind fleet-footed Clancy Diggs.

Chapter Twenty-Seven

"So, let me get this straight. You are opposing my opposition to your being arrested and taken for questioning." Bill loosened his necktie, unbuttoned his shirt, unsnapped his watchband, and slid it over his hand in a matter of seconds. He dropped his watch and ring in a dish on top of the chest of drawers, then added his tie to others layered over a hanger in the closet.

"I wasn't arrested. I'm just asking you to understand."

She flopped down on the bed. "I had no way of knowing there were slot machines in the back room of the supper club. I guess that's where the social part of *I Digg It Supper and Social Club* comes in. Nor had I even an inkling the police were set to raid the place. Had I known, I would have gone with Clancy out the bookcase door."

"I told you Diggs is a snake in the grass. I'm more than a little annoyed that you went to see him."

He hung his trousers on the doorknob in case he had to dress during the night for a burglar or something equally urgent, then put on his robe, and slipped his feet into bedroom shoes. Kissing his wife on top of her head, he sat down beside her. "I'm not angry. I'm upset, honey, because I don't want you to get hurt."

"I know. I can't stop thinking about Marigold. I can't help imagining what may be happening to her." She leaned on his shoulder.

His arm slid around her, and he kissed her curly head again. "I know you are tired. Get ready for bed. I'm going to read for a while."

On her way to take a quick shower, she searched for a fresh gown among neatly folded clothes in a drawer.

"Where's Waldo," she called out the open door, as she dried and dressed. "He missed Charles Pennington's meeting this morning."

"He had to fly to New York on urgent business. The man runs an empire. He should be back by now." Bill looked at the clock on the bedside stand. Ten after ten.

"Mother said Sonya was released from the hospital today. She thinks Rossana will be discharged tomorrow. Klara is staying with her aunt tonight, but they are depending on Waldo to be there tomorrow night."

Jix scuffed barefooted across the carpet and sat down at the dresser. She stared at her reflection in the mirror. Much of the mascara applied hours earlier had relocated to underneath her eyes during the steamy shower. She looked like a raccoon.

"Oh, dear me," she bemoaned. Cold cream dissolved the mascara mask. *If only it were this simple to get rid of the lilac walls*, she thought.

Bill sunk into bed pillows stacked against the headboard and opened a book. He read half a page twice before laying the book aside. "So, Diggs didn't verify the information the quarry man gave you."

"No. I think he may have if a S.W.A.T. team had not blazed through the building and distracted him, as one is prone to be distracted in such lively circumstances." She was tired, and sarcasm was a handy channel to vent her frustrations.

130

Dropping her hairbrush onto the dresser, she turned to face him. "Oh, Bill! What are we going to do? It's been five days. Detective Bird said she would call if they have a definite lead, and I haven't heard a word from her. Waldo has called in every favor he can, and no one has come up with anything other than what Colton said Clancy told him."

"What makes you think the beach house tip is any more reliable than the quarry or the cabin Waldo searched? If we all piled in cars and alerted the police to meet us there, there is nothing to guarantee that Diggs talked with Lisandra or that they are on an island."

"I know," she said, disparaging of hope.

"Let's call it a day. Come to bed, sweetheart. You are exhausted, and I have a busy day tomorrow. I have two closings and a foreclosure scheduled," he sighed. "A start for some, a finish for others. I may be late getting home tomorrow night." He put the book on the table and folded the cover back on her side of the bed.

Jix sank into a cloud of comfort and pulled the blanket around her. Bill turned off the light on his side and scooted over toward her.

"Something good is about to break that will lead us to Marigold. I feel it in my bones," he said.

She snuggled close to him. His words of encouragement melted into her soul. Jix latched onto a sense of peace that chased away uncertainty. Whether he was right or wrong, she chose to believe him. And at that moment, without a single shred of proof, she believed everything would be all right. The magic splendor of sleep cast its spell, and on a wispy cloud, she gently drifted toward the land of sweet dreams.

Bill yawned, turned over, and scooted back-to-back. His words trailed to deaf ears.

"Honey, I just remembered. Theo Somebody is coming tomorrow to paint the room."

Chapter Twenty-Eight

"Good morning, sleepyhead. "Carol repeated a phrase her mother had often spoken to her and her sister, Vicki, when they were little girls. She poured two cups of coffee, added cream and sugar to one, and set them on the table.

"Thanks. Where is everybody?" Jix sipped the hot brew before leaning over to kiss her granddaughter busily chasing cereal bits on the highchair tray. Willowdean lay in wait for a stray oat treat to bounce in her direction.

"Gran went to a meeting at eight. Mr. Pennington is presenting a plan to attempt to undo Bryson's shenanigans. Dad left at seven to preview paperwork for mortgages he is closing on today. Earl is in the shop…I heard the drill running. Do you want toast?"

"Toas'?" said the pint-sized connoisseur of toasted bread frosted with grape jelly.

"You've already had toast and an egg, sweet girl. Mom?"

Jix shook her head. "No, thank you. I'll fix something later." She reached over and stabbed a Cheerio with a licked finger and popped it in her mouth. "I just want to sip a couple of cups of coffee. I assume you are working today."

Carol had twisted her strawberry-blonde, shoulder-length hair into a bun and pinned it at the crown of her head. Looking healthy and wholesome with little to no make-up, tiny hoop earrings, and blue scrubs, she was the perfect picture of a home-healthcare professional. Many of her patients were elderly. Carol not only offered competent medical care, but she always added a dose of cheerfulness and encouragement.

A sweet smile flashed across her face. "Yes, I'm working. I scheduled my first patient for after lunch. I wasn't sure if you were available to take care of Dinah until Gran gets back. I want to stop by and check in on Sonya and Rossana. Sonya for sure; I don't know if Rossana's been discharged"

Jix refilled her cup from a carafe Carol had set on the table. "I guess you heard about last night's fiasco."

A chuckle escaped. "Dad said you and Abby Gayle were arrested inside a shady establishment."

Jix rolled her eyes and answered matter-of-factly, "We were not arrested. We were detained for questioning."

In addition to telling of the previous night's events, she emphasized how they were valued witnesses, in that they had revealed to the police the location of the bookcase door.

"We were dismissed before they found how to open the thing."

Jix took another tiny cereal donut from Dinah.

"Mom, I'll be glad to pop some bread in the toaster."

"I'm not hungry. Just taking advantage of an opportunity to teach Dinah how to share." They laughed together. The toddler hadn't a clue as to what was funny, nor did it matter; she laughed at laughter.

Changing the subject, Jix enquired as to her son-in-law's well being. Scotty would return from his teaching tour soon to retrieve his wife and baby. The dreaded day would arrive far too soon for Jix and Bill.

The subject changed again, this time to the stalemate they'd reached in the ongoing hunt for the family matriarch.

"Something is about to break. We'll find her, Mom. I believe a good outcome is brewing." Carol added more cereal on the tray, tossing a few on the floor for Willowdean.

"You and your dad are two peas in a pod, and I am so grateful to have you both in my life."

Earl knocked on the back door. "Mornin'. Just want to let you know the Agathangelos are here to paint." He held the kitchen door with his foot.

"Now I understand why Bill kept calling the man Theo Somebody."

Jix peeped out to see a van parked in the driveway. Two, tall men wearing white, painter's overalls jabbered in their native language as they gathered tarps, rollers, and brushes. "Nobody ever tells me anything. At least, I made the bed."

The phone rang. "I'll get it." Carol went into the den.

The painters piled into the kitchen with a ton of paint paraphernalia seeking instructions as to where and what to paint. Earl asked Jix about trunks to be worked on, and Carol screamed from the other room, "Mom! Hurry!"

"Excuse me," she said to the painters. "Earl, keep an eye on Dinah, please." She raced to the den.

The television sprang to life with a click of the remote; Carol selected a channel. "That was Abby Gayle on the phone. She's on her way here. Look, Mom! She says this is Lisandra Judd."

"Go get Dinah, honey. Tell Earl to take the painters upstairs." Jix sat down on the sofa, her eyes glued to the television screen.

Local news anchor Angela O'Neill had interrupted *The Price Is Right* to broadcast live coverage of breaking news.

Squinting from sun glare, the familiar newswoman narrated as the cameraman panned to a massive machine in the distance. Repeating information piped through an earpiece, the aging anchorwoman with the same hairstyle she'd worn since the seventh grade described the heavy equipment as a front wheel loader used to load rock that is moved by crawler tractors or blasting technicians.

Weary from waiting for scattered morsels, Willowdean stretched out in a patch of sunshine streaming through the den windows. Carol settled Dinah in her safe play area and hurried to sit down in her father's recliner.

"What's happening?"

The answer was before their eyes. Perched inside the cab of the machine, Lisandra Judd raised and lowered a hydraulic arm attached to a bucket with a capacity of up to thirty-five tons.

She dragged the bucket across rocky ground gathering loose stones and dirt. A shift of the lever, and up the scoop rose like a Ferris wheel gondola. A tilt in the opposite direction and rock rained down.

The cameraman scanned onlookers as Angela spoke in a tone of voice that reflected expressions on the faces of those watching in disbelief.

"Is this taking place at a quarry?"

"Looks like it. There's Colton. It has to be Stonewall Quarry," Jix pointed out a man talking to quarrymen.

"How is it that she can operate a piece of equipment like that?" Carol murmured.

"Lord only knows, but she's handling it like a pro."

A reflective flash off chrome trim distracted Jix. She glanced outside to see Abby Gayle pull into the driveway.

"Did Earl show the painters to lilac land?" Jix asked, without looking away from the TV.

"Yes ma'am." Carol cocked her ear toward the door while following the excitement playing out on the screen. "I hear them moving furniture."

Abby Gayle, gasping as if she'd run instead of driven, rushed in and crashed on the sofa. "This is unbelievable! Have they said anything about Marigold and Aaron?"

"No, but if Lisandra's at the quarry, they must be nearby. We'd better go see."

No sooner had she sat down, Abby Gayle was again on the run. She and Jix darted to the door.

"I'll drive," Jix shouted. She called back to Carol, "Honey, please call Waldo and ask him to meet us there."

Chapter Twenty-Nine

The rutted access road from the main highway in the rear-view mirror, Jix parked and, on foot, she and Abby Gayle darted past news vans and police vehicles adorned with idling, flashing lights

"There's Blanche!" Jix pointed toward a crowded landing outside the trailer door. Curious onlookers craned their necks to get a better view. Diesel exhaust billowed from the stack of a jerking, lurching piece of heavy equipment.

Abby Gayle led the way. "If we hurry, we can get in behind the trailer before they close that area." The two crouched and ducked between cars.

A helicopter, carrying a cameraman leaning precariously forward, hovered overhead like a ceiling fan. Arriving in a cloud of dust, half a dozen armed men clad in body armor spilled from a police van.

Quarry workers gathered beneath the spectator's platform; the deck above was packed with law enforcement personnel. Detectives Bird and Martino watched Lisandra through binoculars.

Jix peeped around a propane tank located behind the trailer. She could see Lisandra shouting from the cab and punching the air with her fist like an urban cowgirl riding a mechanical bull.

Abby Gayle pointed out men huddled near the platform. "There's Colton with other quarry workers."

"Where?"

"That island of yellow hard hats."

"I see Detective Bird on the observation platform. If we're spotted, we'll be thrown out of here, but if we can reach Colton or the detective without drawing attention, we can blend in."

Armed men scattered to strategic points, prepared to fire.

"Oh no! We have to stop them! We can't let them shoot her!"

With no thought of consequences, Jix made a beeline for the platform. Abby Gayle followed.

"Halt!" an officer yelled. "You can't go there!" Others took up the chase.

"Run, Abby Gayle!" Jix called.

"Detective Bird!" Abby Gayle and she screamed and waved their hands as they neared the platform. Colton saw the women and dashed to meet them.

Avonelle Bird turned to investigate the commotion and shouted to let the women pass, then hurried down the stairs. The anchorwoman directed the cameraman to pan in their direction.

Winded, Jix blurted out, "She's delusional! Don't shoot her! Please don't shoot her. She can lead us to Marigold!"

Abby Gayle took up the cause, "She's high on heroin! Only she knows where Marigold and Aaron are! If she is killed, we may never find them! Call off the shooters!"

Bird replied, "I've already thought of that. The shooters are a last resort. We're in control of the situation!"

The giant, earth-moving machine came to a standstill and idled noisily. Apprehension gripped the crowd.

Spewing fumes like an erupting volcano, the powerful

machine lurched forward, clawing the rocky terrain. The observation platform appeared to be Lisandra's likely target.

Everyone scattered like mice.

"We have to stop her before she hurts someone or herself!" Jix grabbed Colton by his shirtsleeve. "She knows you, Colton. If Abby Gayle and I can get in one side of the cab to distract her and you come in the other side, we can stop her."

Colton knew Jix had underestimated the risk. "The sides are open, but if the loader is moving, it'll be a challenge to get on board."

"Send one of your men with another machine to distract her. When she slows down, it'll give us time to get inside."

Detective Bird vehemently resisted. "I can't let you risk injury or worse! My men will do it. Stay out of the way!"

The loader neared at a steady pace.

Jix pled, "If Colton approaches her, she may react less violently. There's no time to debate this! She is the only person who knows where Marigold and Aaron are."

There was no time to block the loader; the massive machine was minutes from plowing head-on into the platform.

"Try your way. We'll back you up!" Bird relented.

The tremendous impact folded support columns like bended knees and transformed what had been a solid deck into a woodpile. Dazed and disoriented, Lisandra grappled with the levers, attempting to find reverse.

"She carries a stiletto," Jix tossed a warning over her shoulder to Colton as she and Abby Gayle ran to the far side of the loader, grabbed on to the handrails, and with a hefty thrust heaved themselves up the steps.

First sight of the shell of a person, who was little more than skin and bones, stunned Jix. The element of surprise tipped the scales, and they easily overpowered her.

Colton lunged in from the opposite side, turned the key to kill the engine, and helped restrain Lisandra. Jix shook the emaciated woman by the shoulders until her head bobbled. "Where is Marigold?" she screamed. "Tell us what you've done with Marigold!"

Abby Gayle pulled her friend away. It was apparent the woman had no presence of mind to answer.

Law enforcement immediately took over, retrieving the stiletto from inside her sleeve.

Lisandra Judd, once a bright, optimistic, gifted woman whose brain had been rewired by drugs, was in the agonizing throes of withdrawal.

Chapter Thirty

Racked with tremors and nausea, Lisandra was rushed to the hospital by ambulance. All but one or two news crews packed their equipment into vans and joined the convoy streaming away from the quarry.

As the crowd thinned, Waldo arrived. He apologized profusely for the delay but was assured there had been nothing he could have done had he been there.

Detective Bird and her crew, quarry workers, the county sheriff, volunteers, and a rescue team had gathered to organize a search of the area. It was lunchtime, and they'd decided to delay for an hour to formulate and organize a practical plan.

Jix, Abby Gayle, and Waldo had no intention of wasting an hour or a minute or a second. They stood by Waldo's car strategizing on their own. Jix remembered when Bill had first mentioned the car phones. "Waldo. Let's try to call Marigold again on your car phone."

Waldo slid behind the steering wheel, Abby Gayle scooted to the middle, and Jix sat in the passenger seat.

He listened to the earpiece happily chirp as he pushed

numbers. "It's busy."

"Busy?"

Perplexed, Jix leaned forward to see around Abby Gayle. "Maybe she is trying to call you."

Waldo hung up, and they waited for his phone to ring, hanging on to the unlikely prospect that Marigold was calling him. They stared at the phone willing it to bring good news.

"She isn't calling me. Her phone must be off the hook. Or Lisandra destroyed it."

Plenty of possibilities as to why they were getting a busy signal were ruled possible but unlikely.

"We can't just sit here. We don't know the area, so we don't know where to look." Jix was antsy. "In the time it'll take to organize a search, we can be well on the way to finding Marigold and Aaron."

Abby Gayle had an idea. "Colton knows the quarry. Let me out. I'll be right back."

Jix opened the door. "I'll go with you. Don't go anywhere, Waldo."

"I'll be here in case the phone rings," he said.

They picked Colton out of a sea of volunteers congregating at the trailer. Abby Gayle pulled him aside, expressed concern at delaying the search, and asked if he would come with her and Jix. Colton put someone else in charge there, leaving word he could be reached on his pager.

The three joined Waldo to discuss a workable plan. Meanwhile, a helicopter carrying deputies from the sheriff's department arrived.

Other than dense growth in small strips of wildlife habitats bordering the six-hundred-acre property, the absence of trees and undergrowth were an advantage. The land was flat with few exceptions, such as open excavated pits and berms that functioned as buffer zones to minimize noise.

Colton pointed over here, over there, while predicting the

searchers would first explore a settling pond, so there was no need for them to look there.

"Where do you suggest we search?" Waldo asked.

Everyone got out of the car so Colton could draw in the dirt with a sharp rock.

"You and I will go over there." Speaking to Waldo, he drew a semicircle, and pointed to *over there*.

"You ladies go this way," he waved in the opposite direction. "We'll circle around and meet back at the observation platform. Once the main search begins, others will join us and cover this area," he drew a large X on the ground.

Colton left to get his truck and come back for Waldo. Jix and Abby Gayle walked to Jix's truck, each struggling with thoughts of an ominous outcome.

Chapter Thirty-One

"We should think ahead to when we find them. Whether that happens today or another day, they will be found." Abby Gayle was concerned for her friend. "I don't want to suggest an unhappy ending, but we should be prepared for anything."

"I know." Her laconic reply implied there was no need for further discussion.

Jix zigzagged around sharp rocks. A dusty blanket settled on the hood and windshield. The wipers whisked away a soupy mixture of muddy washer fluid, leaving a fan-shaped peephole.

A bland color scheme of multihued browns, whites, and grays stretched before them. Islands of massive boulders dotted a Mars-like landscape.

"This vast wasteland is depressing," Abby Gayle looked out the side window. "I need green. I need life."

"I'll second that motion. Give me trees with birds and streams with fish. A little bit of this goes a long way."

The women searched behind random boulders occasionally getting out of the truck to search on foot.

When the plateau ended at a ledge bordering an abandoned

pit that spanned several miles, Jix parked, and they walked to the rim. Shielding their eyes from early afternoon sun, they looked over the edge.

"It's like a canyon. What do you think? Twenty or thirty feet to the bottom?" Jix gazed down a sheer wall of scraped stone.

Abby Gayle guesstimated. "At least. Let's walk. We can't drive close enough to see over."

They stumbled on rocky, uneven ground, frequently peering into the precipice.

When Abby Gayle turned, she was surprised at how far they'd come. "Maybe we should go back and get the truck. We've come farther than it seems."

"Okay," Jix thoughtlessly responded. Her attention was drawn to tracks in a layer of surface soil. She stopped dead still.

"Look at this. There are two sets of tracks."

"What?"

"Over there." She walked toward the impressions. Pointing away from the ledge, she looked down a stretch of tire tracks disappearing in the distance.

Jix whirled around to see where they led.

"I don't see other tire tracks. Do you? I doubt there has been work in this area recently. Why these tracks?" she wondered.

"No. This has to be an abandoned area. As we know, they are working closer to the entrance."

"These tracks are from a loader." Jix said. "Look at the pattern."

"These are clearly car tracks." Abby Gayle pointed out both sets. They stooped to compare the two.

Jix suddenly sprang upright as quickly as a Jack-in-the-box.

"Oh dear God!" she screamed. Her hands flew to her cheeks. "Oh, no! No!" She ran toward the ledge.

"Wait! Wait, Jix." Abby Gayle caught up with her.

"Lisandra has pushed Marigold's car off the ledge!" Jix cried.

Chapter Thirty-Two

"I'll get help!" Abby Gayle shouted. She held her trembling friend at arm's length. "You stay here. Don't do anything stupid like trying to get down there. Promise?"

"I promise." Jix nodded. "Run! Hurry!"

Abby Gayle launched into a sprinter's gait and raced to the truck. Within minutes, the speeding vehicle was but a speck on the horizon.

Jix crept to the rim to view the wreckage amid fallen rock. The long, black, luxury sedan lay like a turtle on its back that had ceased trying to upright itself.

Silence that speaks rose like incense from an altar.

Once Marigold and Aaron were lost, but now they were found. The moment of truth was at hand.

From where Jix stood, there were no apparent signs of life. A broken sob lodged in her throat; a knot in the pit of her stomach tightened until she was nauseated. It was obvious from the wreckage that survival was unlikely.

Even though the outlook did not warrant it, inwardly, she hoped against dwindling hope.

"Until I see Marigold's lifeless body, I will not accept that she is gone!" she shouted, her nails biting into clinched fists. Her chest rose and fell rapidly to the beat of an unfolding awareness of the sacredness of every human life.

Something warm and gentle touched her cheek. Although she blamed her imagination for playing tricks, it was as if an angel had kissed her.

Taking baby steps backwards until she could no longer see below, she slumped to the ground and criss-crossed her legs, rhythmically rocking from side to side. Riding a runaway train of thoughts, Jix dried her face with her shirttail then drew her knees up and rested her head on them.

The tire tracks came to mind. These tread marks could not only prove the car had been pushed over the ledge, but forensics would be able to tie the treads to a specific machine. Having enough presence of mind to know when help arrived they would unknowingly destroy the evidence, Jix walked alongside for several yards, then took off her top shirt, shoes, socks, and spread them on the ground to flag the spot. Her efforts would attract attention and deter drivers but not guarantee the tracks were protected.

Placing rocks as large as she could carry, she added to the border. Working quickly, she had sectioned off a lengthy stretch when far away, Colton's truck emerged ahead of a caravan of search volunteers, quarry workers, news people, and standby EMTs.

A whirlybird swooped past and lowered near the wreckage, settling deliberately like a nesting hen.

Jix flagged Colton and his passengers, Waldo and Abby Gayle. An explanation of the need to protect the tire tread evidence prompted Colton and Waldo to mark the area with neon tape Colton had in his truck. They knew that in spite of their efforts, some could trample inside the boundaries, and rotor wind might erase the impressions. Regardless of the end result, they had made an admirable attempt to preserve evidence at a crime scene.

Detectives and law enforcement personnel gathered. A news helicopter hovered in the vicinity; additional paramedics arrived on the scene and were quickly directed to an access road.

Before preparations to turn the vehicle upright could be implemented, rescuers pried a door open.

Jix, Abby Gayle, and Waldo watched from the ledge as the limp body of Marigold was pulled from the wreckage. She lay motionless, her hands and feet bound, her mouth duct taped.

Feeling faint and light-headed, Jix looked away. "Oh, dear God."

Waldo put his arm around her shoulder and the other around Abby Gayle. The three huddled for both physical and emotional support.

Colton told them of an access road that led to the lower plateau. He asked them to wait until he'd talked with medical responders. Jix begged to go with him, but he insisted she wait. Waldo and Abby Gayle knew they would be in the way and reasoned with Jix, convincing her to stay with them.

An eternity passed until the little band of anxious onlookers watched Colton return to fetch Waldo and Jix to accompany Marigold to the hospital in the rescue helicopter.

"Thank God she's alive." Jix and Abby Gayle were euphoric when Colton delivered the good news.

Waldo sensed the weight of agonizing days and sleepless nights lifting. Caught in a whirlpool of emotions, he laughed and cried.

The closer Colton and his passengers came to the wreckage, the more desperately they yearned to see for themselves that Marigold was indeed alive and perhaps even conscious. Try as they might, it was impossible to determine anything more than that emergency workers were preparing to transport. The three anxiously waited in the truck to be summoned for an imminent departure.

Jix and Waldo boarded the aircraft when the patient was safely inside. Medical personnel gave a guarded report of Marigold's condition.

When buckled in, Waldo leaned to speak quietly to Jix. "They don't know the extent of her injuries." He squeezed her hand. "But she is alive," he smiled and repeated, "she's alive."

The bird's noisy, whapping blades whipped up a rush of wind and dust as it ascended to the clouds. Soon as they were out of sight, Colton would go back for Abby Gayle and drive her to be with the others at the hospital.

As they lifted off, Jix stared down at Aaron Williams' lifeless body covered with a white sheet, lying near the wreckage.

Chapter Thirty-Three

"So, let me get this straight," Bill Haynes was relieved. "You do like the blue?" He presented a rhetorical question.

"I do," she answered. Jix looked around the very blue room. "I do," she repeated, as if convincing herself. "Much better than the lilac. Do you like it?"

"Yes. It's regal. Sophisticated." He beamed as if he'd correctly answered the final Jeopardy question. This was, after all, his choice of color.

She laughed. "You sound like that realtor we met at the open house last month. To hear her tell it, everything looks regal if you have a regal outlook."

Nightclothes draped over her arm, Jix went into the bathroom. "This may qualify as the longest day of my life. I feel like a wet noodle," she called out the open door. "But thank God, Marigold is alive and in good hands."

"I know what you mean." He sat on the bed and pulled off his shoes. "And not everyone's wife made both the six and ten o'clock news. What a lucky fellow I am. Angela O'Neill must be as happy as a lark." A shoe dropped.

"I do what I can," she quipped.

She'd taken the quickest shower on record and returned to sit down at the dresser.

"I am so grateful we have Marigold with us again..." she swallowed a lump, "...and so sorry to lose Aaron. Mother and Eva are staying at the hospital tonight. Waldo too, I think. Or he may have gone to stay with Rossana and Sonya." She brushed her chin-length hair with steady strokes.

Bill headed for the shower. "Did Austin make it home? Abby Gayle will have plenty to tell him."

"She called and said they were ordering pizza and staying in tonight."

"She's a trooper, isn't she?"

"The best friend on earth. I don't know what I would do without her."

The phone rang. Jix scurried to the bedside table hoping Dinah had not awakened.

It was Margee with the final update of the day. Marigold was conscious, and, albeit feebly, she was talking a mile a minute. So far, she had been diagnosed with dehydration, high blood pressure, a broken wrist, and multiple abrasions and burns from airbag deployment. None of these were her main concern.

Root touch-up was her highest priority. Waldo had seen her with gray roots. She'd asked for a surgical cap to wear until her hairdresser could perform a bit of magic.

Bill came from the bathroom, reclaimed his shoes from where they'd landed, and slid them under the bed. "Did I hear the phone ring?"

"It was Mother with wonderful news. Marigold is practically unscathed. She doesn't appear to have serious head or internal injuries. Her stamina is phenomenal. Even though she was bound, Lisandra had fastened her seat belt...from force of habit, I suppose. They surmise the car hit and flipped in such a way that the initial impact was lessened. Possibly the air bag saved her life."

"And Aaron?"

She paused reflectively. "An autopsy will reveal the cause of death. Marigold says he had died during the night; she thinks of natural causes. He was not well before this whole thing began. He'd been recently diagnosed with early signs of heart failure."

"Let's call it a day." He pulled back the covers on his side and slipped into bed.

"Oh, Lord, how sweet it is," he moaned, as muscles relaxed.

She surveyed the room before turning off the bedside lamp. "I do like the blue paint, but the room still needs something. We'll have to get new drapes and a bedspread. Maybe I'll have the chaise lounge recovered, too. What do you think about wallpapering one wall?"

She answered her question before he did, "Yes. Wallpaper. I'll paper one wall. And different lamps, too…slowly, but surely, we're getting there. A few tweaks and everything will be perfect."

"I'd like to hope so."

Bill pulled the cover under his chin and turned toward the wall. "Get in bed, sweetheart. The longest day of our lives has finally come to an end."

She switched off the light.

Chapter Thirty-Four

"More coffee, Dad?" Carol, wearing pink scrubs, set a scrambled egg before a hungry toddler chewing bacon. Dinah's close associate, Willowdean, had eaten and then curled up on a rug to snooze.

"If you don't mind," Bill stuck his cup in her direction without looking up from the morning newspaper. "Thanks. Has everyone seen the front page? Quarry owner Clancy Diggs says the cause of the accident is yet to be determined. There is an ongoing investigation."

Jix sliced a banana over a bowl of cereal. "That's pretty much all the police have released, too. Detective Bird has asked us not to comment to the media. She'll have a news conference today or tomorrow."

Toasted bread popped up. Margee slathered both slices with butter and dropped in two more. "Marigold wants to talk to you and Abby Gayle, Jix."

"We're going to see her this morning."

Carol scraped the last of the egg and licked it off her coffee spoon. "My concern is for Lisandra. Drug addiction is horrible, and withdrawal is like the flu times ten. Mom says Clancy told them she became addicted after a serious injury."

Jix said between bites, "Morphine then heroin."

"Herion is an opioid made from morphine. The substance comes from the poppy plant. If what Mom told me that Clancy told her and Abby Gayle is accurate, Lisandra has been using for years. She no longer uses to get high; she uses to stave off the physical and psychological tug-of-war associated with withdrawal." Carol poured herself more coffee. "It is no surprise she is paranoid and delusional. I'd be surprised if she wasn't. She needs help, and I hope she gets it."

Jix sipped coffee before commenting. "When I first saw her, I was shocked. She looked like death warmed over."

Carol said, "Some think if an addict would just stop using, they could get off drugs. Oh, how I wish it were that simple. Drugs alter healthy brain function. They cause shallow breathing, and less oxygen to the brain can cause brain damage. Inflammation to the brain can result in a build up of protein that produces a form of dementia. I have all the compassion in the world for an addict."

"Interesting," said Bill. "And enlightening."

"Why did she take Marigold and Aaron," Margee asked. Two overlooked pink curlers perched on the crown of her head. "Was her plan to keep them forever? In light of what Carol just told us, I guess Lisandra didn't have a plan."

Bill and Carol had already discussed Lisandra's motivation. He repeated their conclusions, "Aaron could drive her to get drugs. Marigold was her money source. She knew street dealers. All they had to do was drive up and make a transaction from the car."

Carol added, "Some addicts have more self-control than others; she may have had a plan. This woman was an army nurse. She is military-trained, highly motivated, and capable of executing a plan. This is so sad. Lisandra is also a victim.

Pain from her injuries was so intense, her need for relief led to addiction. It's a catch-22."

Bill pushed his chair away from the table and reached for Dinah. Carol released the highchair tray, and the cherub-faced little girl stretched her arms for him to take her. "Again, thank God Marigold is safe. This could have ended more tragically than it has."

With Dinah on his hip, he said to Jix, "Tell Marigold I'll stop by on my way home around six. For now, my sidekick and I are going to hang out with Mr. Rogers until time for me to leave for work."

He kissed a happy baby as they strolled into the den. Willowdean tagged along, settling in her comfortable bed on the fireplace hearth.

Margee stacked dishes. "I'll be here all day unless someone needs me elsewhere. Eva and I will be making funeral arrangements for Aaron to be held day after tomorrow." She opened the dishwasher. "I want to cook something today that has to simmer all day...I think, spaghetti sauce. Is everyone okay with spaghetti and meatballs?" All were in favor. "Cooking will be good therapy. Waldo will join us at seven. I want to spend the day with Dinah, gather my thoughts, and ease back into my normal routine."

"If you need something from the store, make a list and send Earl to get it," Jix said. "I'll ask him to check with you."

Carol was ready to leave for work. Jix had two hours to actively pursue her Trunk Doctor role.

Carol transferred her lunch from the fridge to a canvas tote bag. "Gran, did you tell Marigold about Bryson and his antics?"

"She asked if anything had taken place she would want to know about. As tactfully as possible, I said that with dubious intentions, Bryson had mishandled a bit of Foundation business, and Charles was looking into it. I didn't elaborate."

Jix put a banana peel in the compost bin and her cup in the

sink. "How'd she react?"

"She referred to the man as a loathsome pimple on the chin of life, whom she's never liked and said when she sees him, she is going to strangle him with her bare hands."

They roared with laughter.

Marigold was home and back to the business of being Marigold.

Chapter Thirty-Five

Hugging a curve, Jix cruised toward a four-story, stucco building towering above the trees. Located on the outskirts of town, the hospital anchored a medical community of doctors ranging from family physicians to a variety of specialists. Pharmacies and fast food restaurants also populated the area.

"Which trunk are you working on?" Abby Gayle propped her elbow on the window ledge. Her short, dark hair fluttered in the wind.

Jix slowed to a stop at an intersection before answering, "The navy blue steamer. Adding fabric to a drawer is risky business. The thickness of the fabric and how well it adheres to wood determines whether the drawer will ever fit properly again. I won't know if it will open and close easily until the glue dries. I have my fingers crossed."

"At least you've made progress. If there's anything I can do to help, just ask. Austin will be here for the rest of this week then he has a short run to Florida. I may go with him."

Jix turned into the parking deck. "You should. You'll have fun and it'll give you and Austin time together…not to mention the opportunity to show off a new bikini."

"Right," she laughed. "That would be a show all right. I'll stick to my one-piece with a flouncy skirt. It's really cute and I'm cute wearing it."

They stopped at the gift shop and chose books and candy for Marigold. She was sleeping when they arrived but happy to be awakened.

Margee had said there was bruising. She had not mentioned the extent of blackened eyes, emphasized by freckled, pale skin. A brace encased a mending wrist. An orange silk scarf wrapped turban-style around her head and knotted in front hid outgrown roots, the bane of any colored-hair gal's existence. To complete the Marigold-look, diamond-studded ear lobes competed with fire-engine-red lips.

Lady Fairmont was a wonderful, loveable, precious sight to her guests. The women hugged, shed more than a few tears, and shared praises for Marigold's return and sadness that Aaron had not been as fortunate. At her urging, the visitors pulled up chairs to listen.

She began at Lisandra's sudden appearance, their abduction, leaving Rossana behind, going through the tunnel to Aaron's, and each and every day since. Marigold stopped several times to rest while Jix and Abby Gayle asked questions or told how they had searched for her.

They also recounted their visit with Diggs. "The club was raided, and Clancy Diggs was no longer available to tell us anything more."

Marigold asked Jix to raise the head of the bed. Once she was comfortable, she launched into her major concern,

"That's who I want to discuss with you two, Clancy Diggs. From many things Lisandra said, I think Clancy put her up to stabbing the Shepherd sisters and kidnapping me. And I think he intended for her to murder every one of us."

"What did she say that left you with that impression?" Abby

Gayle asked.

Marigold took a sip of juice and set the cup back on a tray. "Lisandra behaved erratically a great deal of the time, but there were periods when she was quite lucid. Long before she became unhinged, I suspected Clancy was fueling a rivalry between Lisandra and the Shepherd sisters."

Talking rapidly in typical Marigold fashion, she rendered her opinion, "If I were in the market for a man, I'd walk all over Clancy Diggs looking for the right one. I wouldn't put anything past that sawed-off-low-life-sorry-excuse for a man. Lisandra became increasingly paranoid. None of us had romantic feelings for Clancy…he should be so lucky. The more we attempted to reason with her, the more obsessive she became."

Abby Gayle took advantage of a pause and quickly jumped in, "Clancy expressed genuine concern for Lisandra and claimed they were old friends. Why would he turn her against you?"

"Well, first and foremost, because Clancy acted genuinely concerned doesn't mean he was concerned at all. He wanted you to think he was concerned for her welfare when the truth is his primary concern is always for his welfare. He is a pathological liar and a thief, and Lord only knows what else! I wouldn't put anything past him. If he cast blame on Lisandra, he lied to you, and my guess is he did it with a straight face. Don't feel badly that you fell for it. Clancy can be very convincing; he is an actor. The Shepherd sisters met him in a regional theatre group. This is all his doing! I don't know his motive, but I'm convinced he wanted us all dead. Lisandra failed when she only wounded the sisters, and she delayed harming me even when Clancy encouraged her. She talked with him every day on my car phone. Aaron and I overheard each conversation…her end of it, that is. She couldn't work the blasted gadget, and I had to get him on the phone each time."

Marigold took a deep breath and paused to reflect on one-sided conversations she and Aaron had attempted to decipher.

"Aaron and I were too valuable to her. Perhaps that was our saving grace, or perhaps Lisandra is not a killer at heart. She threatened to harm Aaron if I didn't give her money, and to harm me if he didn't do as she said. When upset, she wielded that knife like she was Norman Bates. Either Aaron or I were restrained at all times. As the days passed, we were convinced that Clancy put her up to this whole thing." Breathless, she paused for a moment.

"But why?" The mystery kept surfacing.

"I've known Clancy for two years." Momentarily overcome with a wave of breathlessness, Marigold looked away from her visitors. She inhaled deeply and stared overhead at the light fixture.

Latching on to a second wind, she continued, "He's a wealthy man. How he makes his money is questionable, but nevertheless, he is wealthy. I've never had a cross word with him even though I've never liked him. I know Stacy and Shaleece to be lovely people. For the life of me, I can't think why he would want Lisandra to harm them." As an afterthought, she added, "Or me."

"It will be helpful if we can find a motive." Jix took Marigold's hand. Moved with compassion, she said, "If you'd like to rest, we can talk again later."

"No. No, this is important. Just bear with me...bruised lung, or something of the sort. I'm a little short on air, but there's plenty out there if I can manage to take it in." To minimize discomfort, she took shallow breaths. "What do you think? Has all this happened because Clancy stirred up a hornet's nest?"

"Well, if he provoked her, he is as guilty as Lisandra for what she's done, and he should be held accountable also." All agreed with Abby Gayle.

"She's going to jail for assault or attempted murder and kidnapping. We have to determine if he used Lisandra. And, if he did, we have to prove it," Jix stated.

"Did you talk with Detective Bird about your suspicions?" Abby Gayle asked.

"No," Marigold answered. "It is an assumption on my part. I could be wrong…I was *once* before," she laughed herself into a painful coughing spell. Regaining composure, she added, "I want you two to look into this before I discuss my suspicions with Detective Bird."

Abby Gayle spoke to Jix, "We may have to pay another visit to the mysterious Mr. Diggs."

"First, let's drop in on the Shepherd sisters. Marigold, where can we find them?"

Chapter Thirty-Six

A few phone calls and Marigold located the Shepherds recuperating at an extended care facility. Bearing gifts of flowers and books, Jix and Abby Gayle called on the siblings as ambassadors sent by Marigold.

The sisters looked to be related about as much as giraffes and hamsters. Stacy was blue-eyed, petite, with thin, golden hair unlike Shaleece, her brown-eyed, full-figured, sibling with a head of thick, brunette locks.

Both sisters were delighted to meet Jix and Abby Gayle and thrilled at an update on Marigold. They hadn't heard about Aaron and were saddened by his passing.

"Where is Lisandra?" Stacy asked.

Jix wasn't certain. "She was arrested and is hopefully receiving help for her addiction. Marigold is being discharged in the morning. Aaron's funeral is tomorrow afternoon. But what about you, ladies? How are you?"

Shaleece, the more seriously injured of the two, swung her feet to the floor and sat on the side of the bed. "Lucky to be alive. Both of us."

Stacy narrated the horrific incident and shared how close she'd come to death from wounds primarily to the shoulders and mid-torso.

Showing off her bandaged hands, Shaleece told how she had lost a finger when she'd attempted to take the stiletto from their assailant.

Jix boldly asked, "Do you mind sharing with us how this all came about? Marigold has a theory you may be interested in hearing, but first, was there a specific incident that provoked Lisandra? You were all sharing an apartment, right?"

"Yes," Stacy, only able to sit up for short intervals, turned to face the visitors. "Lisandra came to live with us when Clancy Diggs offered to rent a three bedroom condo. He said he was concerned that she lived alone and thought the three of us would get along, so we moved in together at his insistence."

Shaleece added an interesting element, "He conveniently neglected to tell us Lisandra was a drug addict. From the day she moved in, there was friction."

"Because of her addiction?" Abby Gayle assumed the obvious.

"That and jealousy. She felt we were vying for Clancy. Both Stacy and I had dated him a few times, but we also went out with other men; there was never anything exclusive with Clancy."

Jix hesitated to ask, but she wanted to know, so explaining that no offense was intended, she barged ahead, "He was paying the rent. What did he get in return?"

Abby Gayle readied to make a rapid exit, certain she and Jix were about to be asked to leave.

Stacy laughed. "Not what you'd think. I'm a paralegal, and I'd done research for Clancy. We struck a deal that he would pay for a condo as restitution."

"May I ask what you researched?"

"I signed a non-disclosure agreement. I've agreed not to reveal the kind of research or the findings. Clancy would be furious that I've told you he paid the rent. I didn't even tell the police."

"Of course. You are bound to that agreement. It's just that there are so many questions as to Clancy's involvement with Lisandra and Lisandra's vicious attack on you. Marigold thinks Clancy promoted jealousy as a means of pushing her to a point of violence. Why he would do such a thing is perplexing, to put it mildly."

Stacy and Shaleece exchanged knowing looks. Several seconds passed before Stacy said, "I know a contract cannot be enforced if the contracted activities are felonies. Were that the case, I would be free to discuss with you my business dealings with Mr. Diggs."

"Not knowing what you researched, I would be unable to say if such information contributed to a felony offense. But must we not also consider that we are talking girl-talk—a bit of chummy chitchat? What is said in this room stays in this room." Jix zipped her lips with her fingers.

Lisandra was the obvious perpetrator, but had she been a puppet at the mercy of a master puppeteer?

Women's intuition, that bridge between instinct and reason, is a magical, internal force that prevails primarily in women to alert when something isn't as it appears. This asset is invaluable when raising children. All four women had a gut feeling that Clancy was up to no good. They also had long since learned that when united, women could achieve anything once they put their minds to it. Everyone present had a burning desire to see all who had inflicted hurt, pain, and lies pay.

Stacy tired easily. Her visitors offered to come again another day, but she bravely insisted they stay. Shaleece sipped from a straw in a drink that Abby Gayle held for her before she eased back onto pillows and propped her bandaged hands on the bed tray.

And then, when all were settled, just as pretty as you please, sister Stacy dropped a bombshell.

"Clancy wanted research done by someone outside his network so there would be no record of payments. When I agreed to do the work, he suggested he rent the condo as payment for my services."

"What subject did you research?" Abby Gayle asked.

"How to dissolve a nonprofit foundation. How to transfer assets."

"Well, well," was all a stunned Jix could manage to say. She stared at her hands folded in her lap. "Well, well."

Thrown for a loop by this shocking revelation, Jix could not think clearly. When nothing else came to mind, she mumbled, "As someone once said, 'the plot thickens'."

"What are you saying?" Stacy asked.

"I don't know where this is headed, but I think we are on to something big. Evidently, Lisandra Judd is not the only one the cagey Mr. Diggs has manipulated."

Abby Gayle noted, "Clancy Diggs appears to have more dirt in his business ventures than rocks in his quarry."

Chapter Thirty-Seven

Nests of perfectly placed, flaming-red, curls with touched up roots framed Marigold's tear-stained face. Her friend, Marla, had artfully applied makeup to help conceal bruises around her eyes.

Family and friends went from Aaron's memorial service to Marigold's apartment. Sonya had prepared food to serve with dishes prepared by friends and residents of the building. She and Rossana lovingly doted over Marigold, so grateful to have her home.

Aaron's brother Seth had come to take Aaron to Ohio to be buried in the family plot. As the day came to a close, wake attendees dwindled to a few. Waldo and Eva escorted Seth to the house to gather his brother's personal belongings. It had been decided that Nelda the cat would stay with Eva until arrangements were made for the perfect forever home.

Juliet and Dan Pratt kept the younger Watson children and Dinah during the memorial service. Belinda retrieved Jerry and Jennalee and went to her apartment, leaving the older boys who'd attended the service, to help Sonya tidy up and put the food away.

Carol had gotten her daughter from Juliet and gone to the top floor, knowing that a dose of Dinah would be good medicine for Marigold.

"Go-dee!" Dinah squealed, throwing her arms around Marigold's neck.

"Careful of Goldie's boo-boo," Carol cautioned to not touch Marigold's broken wrist.

"Oh, how sweet it is to hear this precious angel say Goldie." She left red lipstick prints on the child's cheeks. "I have missed you my darling." It had become Goldie's mission in life to see that Dinah had all the love, attention, and toys the little girl would ever want or need.

Bill and Austin said their good-byes; the fellows had plans to hurry to the Haynes' den to catch the last half of the football game.

As Bill backed from a parking space in the lot behind the building, he and Austin spotted a man climbing the fire escape. He pulled alongside the walkway to the front entrance and parked, leaving Austin to deal with anyone objecting to his unorthodox parking methods while he ducked in Eva's to call Jix.

Rossana answered and promptly called Jix to the phone. "Just want to let you know we spotted someone on the fire escape. A man went in a window on the ninth floor. I called Detective Bird and told her," Bill said. "She's either sending someone, or she's on her way."

Jix tactfully avoided promising Bill she'd not get involved, and then rushed to tell Abby Gayle what Bill had seen. "Let's take the stairs and see if we find anyone."

Abby Gayle sprang to her feet, "We should wait for the police or at least take someone with us."

"Bill called Bird. I assume they are coming or sending someone. Let's go down the stairs and wait."

Jonathan, collecting cups and plates from bookcases and tabletops, overheard. Setting aside what he had gathered, he tapped Jix on the shoulder. "I need to talk to you," he leaned in to say.

He led Jix into the hallway. James and Abby Gayle followed.

"What?" James asked.

"I don't have time to talk to you," Jonathan barked at his brother. "Just listen. Miss Jix, I know who came in the window. Please. Don't let them hurt him," he pled.

"Jonathan, calm down. Let's step into the foyer." Jix went first.

"Slow down so we can understand. What are you saying?" Abby Gayle gently patted the fretful youngster's back.

"Just follow me. We don't want to scare him…and let me do the talking. If the police are on the way, we can't waste time."

Jonathan hurried to the end of the foyer opposite the elevator, motioning for the others to keep up. Down the stairs they went, making every effort to heed their leader's prompting to be as quiet as possible.

When Jonathan stepped onto the ninth floor landing, he shouted, "Ryan! Ryan! It's me, Jonathan. Where are you? Don't be afraid."

Jix, Abby Gayle, and James waited at the top of the stairwell as Jonathan walked the corridor calling to the hideaway.

"Ryan. Come out. It's okay. I have friends with me. And my brother…I want you to meet my brother James. Come out. Please."

The door to apartment 9-C opened a few inches.

Jonathan approached and spoke to the eye peeking out. "Hey, Ryan. How you doing?"

The door opened wider, and a tall, straw-haired young man came into view. Jonathan pushed the door open and reached for the man, assuring him it was safe to step outside.

It was obvious the fellow trusted the boy, as he slowly

emerged, glancing about, ready to flee on a second's notice. Jonathan motioned for the others to come and meet his friend. The younger Watson brother handled introductions. Everyone greeted the shy fellow, articulating how pleased they were to make his acquaintance.

At the far end of the hall, the elevator door slid open, and out stepped Detectives Bird and Martino. Ryan darted inside the apartment and closed the door.

"What's going on?" asked Avonelle Bird. "Do we have an intruder?"

Jonathan admitted for the past two months he had helped Ryan, a homeless man who had discovered an unusual way into the building. He sought shelter at night and sometimes slept in the basement where Jonathan left food for him.

"Why didn't you tell me?" James asked.

"I just didn't. You would have told me to tell Miss Eva," he answered. "I found him sleeping in the basement. Well, he wasn't sleeping when I found him, but he'd just woke up when I surprised him. He's not like everybody else. He's…he's a little slow to catch on, but he's not dangerous or anything like that. Please don't hurt him."

Detective Bird said they would do him no harm as long as the man cooperated.

Jonathan tried the knob. The door was locked.

"Ryan, listen to me. It's all right. We're friends, aren't we?" he spoke loudly.

Detective Bird sent Martino outside to be certain the man didn't leave by the fire escape.

Jix stepped up and lightly tapped on the door. "Ryan. You've done nothing wrong. You are not in any trouble. Come out, please, so we can talk. Or if Jonathan and I may come in, unlock the door."

A faint click and a rattle echoed a wave of relief to the anxious listeners. Jonathan opened the door. He and Jix went in and

174

soon returned with Ryan in tow.

"Maybe you'd like something to eat or drink." Abby Gayle thought he might be hungry. She'd grown up hearing her mother say the way to a man's heart was through his stomach. "Miss Fairmont lives on the floor above us." She pointed to the ceiling. "She's had a few people in for refreshments, and I know she has leftovers." Abby Gayle flashed a help-me-out expression to the others.

"There's lots of food," James jumped in. "She has little roast beef sandwiches and chicken sandwiches too."

Jonathan added, "He would know, Ryan. I saw him eat six."

James chuckled. "And I enjoyed every one of them."

Jix put on a warm smile. "Ryan, would you like to join us? There's plenty for everyone. Mrs. Pratt sent a chocolate cake that is out-of-this-world good." The young fellow's face lit up. Chocolate cake was the cross over point.

Detective Bird cheerfully stated to Jonathan's friend, "Excellent idea! I'll go too, if you don't mind. I missed lunch today, and I'm hungry as a bear." Jix put her arm around Bird's shoulder to show Ryan that the policewoman was a friend and not to be feared.

The tall man with innocent, brown eyes and tousled hair never looked anyone but Jonathan in the eye nor did he verbally accept their invitation.

Jonathan reached for Ryan's arm, and the two led the way to the stairwell.

Chapter Thirty-Eight

"So, let me get this straight." Bill threw another pillow over his shoulder, centered it on others stacked against the headboard, and scooted back until he comfortably reclined. "This young man has been hiding in Fairmont Manor?"

Tying the sash on her robe, Jix went into the closet. Through the opened door, she replied, "Not exactly hiding. He needed somewhere safe to sleep. He told us he'd noticed there were no lights at night, or signs of life from outside, on the sixth or ninth floors. On an off chance that a window might be unlocked, he tried until he found one on the ninth floor."

"That was smart." Bill reached for his reading glasses on the bedside table.

Jix came from the closet with two blouses on hangers. Standing before a cheval mirror, she held one up, then the other.

"Carol thinks he may be autistic. She also says there's no one-size-fits-all; there are different types of autism. My general impression was favorable. Ryan is intelligent enough. He lacks social skills. He is slow to speak and to the point when he does."

"Anyone who can climb to those heights has to be capable,

as well as brave ...and we must also factor in he's shown extraordinary determination. Does he have family?"

"Not anymore. His mother passed away several months ago. He couldn't pay rent, so he sold what possessions he had and has been on his own ever since." She disappeared into the closet.

"Tell me again about Rossana. This is unbelievable." He reconsidered reading and laid the book and his glasses on the bedside stand.

Jix came out and sat down at the dressing table.

"We all were startled by his reaction when Rossana came from the kitchen. Marigold had asked Sonya to make Ryan a plate of food. Rossana brought it to him. Based on his response, Detective Bird was prepared to stop him if he attempted to harm her, but he had no ill intentions. He was surprised when he saw her, and I mean pleasantly surprised. Joyfully surprised."

Jix recounted Ryan's story of how he had hidden when he heard the elevator open and three women stumble out. Lisandra, issuing orders, held Marigold at knifepoint while Rossana led the way. An argument turned into a scuffle. Rossana ran, tripped, and hit her head.

"Ryan saw the whole thing?" Bill watched from across the room as Jix rubbed lotion on her hands and arms.

"He was hidden, but he saw everything. He didn't know what to do. Marigold and Lisandra disappeared down the opening to the tunnel. He was concerned Lisandra would reappear, so he hurried to hide Rossana behind the mattress, thinking he was protecting her. He saw the card she'd dropped, and he left others so she would be found."

Bill yawned as he rearranged the pillows and slid down to a supine position. "Being as he was sleeping in the basement, I assume he knew of the mattress and how to get to it easily."

"Apparently so. He left the building after he'd hidden her. He was closer to the elevator than the stairs, or he would have taken them."

"It was him who knocked over the metal cylinder and escaped in the elevator when you and Abby Gayle found Rossana?" Bill turned the bedside light off.

"Right. Then down the fire escape. He came back after the police had searched the building. Ryan thought Rossana had died, just as Abby Gayle and I had...thus his startled response when she walked into the room." Jix giggled at a mental image of Ryan seeing Rossana.

"Lord have mercy! You can't make this stuff up," Bill muttered.

"No, you can't. And Detective Bird heard all this. I forgot to tell you Detective Martino had rejoined us. He heard Ryan's story too."

"All's well that ends well." He closed his eyes.

"Here's the happy part. Waldo and Eva returned from sending Aaron's brother on his journey. Marigold and Waldo discussed the practicality of Ryan staying in Aaron's house. They offered him housing for the time being. He was so grateful, and Jonathan was ecstatic. Sonya sent enough food to last Ryan for days. And guess what?" She was beaming.

"What?"

"Ryan loves cats. It was love at first sight."

"Miracles never cease," he quipped. "Helga and Ryan."

"Nelda and Ryan," she corrected.

Chapter Thirty-Nine

As requested, Jix and Abby Gayle arrived at Marigold's at ten o'clock sharp. Marigold was dressed in a teal outfit that included matching shoes, jewelry, and a shoulder sling for her healing wrist.

She'd asked Jix to drive her new car purchased by telephone and delivered by the local Lincoln dealer. Marigold had not specified their destination. She invited the ladies to help themselves to coffee and scones while she made a phone call.

"Jix, honey, please get my purse off my bed. This call will only take a minute. I need to verify a minor detail with Wally before I share good news." She scooted her well-rounded derriere onto a bench attached to an Art Deco, glass-top telephone table.

Abby Gayle held a napkin underneath a scone as she nibbled her way into the bedroom. Looking at walls papered from floor to ceiling in rich, dark blue and gold, she remarked, "This is the same paper we found in the trunk." She looked closely at the open, web-like gold pattern with visible spaces of blue. "It is beautiful, but these two rooms are somewhat disconnected. They don't blend with the decor in the rest of the house. I would say this is a damask rose pattern, wouldn't you? Do you like it?"

Jix picked up the purse off the bed. "I've always loved this paper. As a child, I loved coming here, and these rooms were my favorite part. The paper is so elegant, so unusual. It's rich and beautiful. The pattern has a hidden charm; I think Bill used the word regal. Recently, I saw a documentary on the Palace of Versailles and other French landmarks where gold gilding is used extensively. It was a very interesting program with information about gold and why it is so valuable."

"It doesn't corrode." Abby Gayle sat down in a chair to finish off the scone.

"Right. A documentary tour guide pointed out wall coverings, door and window frames, moldings, statues, and ornamental carvings all gilded with real gold. These rooms have a *French flair*, don't you think?"

"You should paper a wall in your bedroom if Marigold will share one or two rolls." She licked her finger and captured a few crumbs in her lap. "I'd love to see the Hall of Mirrors at Versailles. Well, of course, the Eiffel Tower and Notre Dame. And visiting Claude Monet's home is a must...and the Louvre and all the museums and fashion houses." A flight of ideas escalated. "We should vacation there. Let's plan to go next summer," Abby Gayle said, with a burst of enthusiasm.

She had sparked Jix's interest. "Bill and Austin included, or you just thinking of a girly getaway?"

Abby Gayle thought for a few seconds. "May as well take them, I guess. Austin is good at directions and finding places. He could come in handy. No-nonsense Bill will keep us out of trouble. We'll have fun."

"I'd love to see France. Then it is settled. Let's seriously plan to go. Bill has a passport; I'll have to get one."

"Us too."

"For now, we have to tie up a few loose ends here. I wonder what Marigold has up her sleeve?"

When Marigold had finished her phone conversation, Jix mentioned the rolls of wallpaper she'd found in the trunk and said she would return them.

"Just keep the wallpaper, honey, if you can use it. Maybe a fancy trunk is in your future. My last year of college I came home for the summer to discover Daddy had the bedroom, sitting room, and hallway papered. Mother thought it was a bit over done, and it is, but whatever Daddy wanted, she supported. Keep the paper and put it to good use. There are several additional rolls in my closet...perhaps as many as a dozen."

"I've been thinking of papering one wall in our bedroom," Jix brought Marigold up to date on the lilac redo.

Abby Gayle commented, "I think the paper will complement the blue paint in your bedroom, Jix, and as Marigold has suggested, paper a trunk."

Marigold continued her story, "I assume Daddy had so many rolls printed to be certain they didn't run short...better-safe-than-sorry sort of thing. The paper was crafted according to his specifications. My interior designer wanted to change it when I redecorated, but I couldn't bear to see it taken down. The paper is homage to my parents." Memories sparkled in dreamy eyes. "If you need more, you know where to find it."

Marigold's arm rested comfortably in the teal sling. Her transformation from bound hostage with silver roots to perfectly fashion-coordinated was tantamount to a caterpillar becoming a butterfly.

"Thank you, Marigold. It will be a perfect addition to my bedroom redo. What are your plans for today? Where are we going?"

"We're going to have a little chat with Clifford Purefoy. He isn't expecting us. Hopefully, by the time we get there, Bryson will be gone; I'd like to talk to his grandfather alone. If not, we'll chat with him too." She took her purse in her *good* hand and walked toward the door.

"Oh," Marigold turned to face them. "I talked to Waldo, and he has been successful in obtaining a long-term, court mandated, live-in drug treatment plan for Lisandra. His lawyer presented her as a veteran with a service record of gallantry in saving patients from a fire when she was stationed in the Philippines. She will get the care she needs. Waldo will see to it. Eventually, she'll be held accountable for what she has done, but we'll help her any way we can."

"That is marvelous news!" The women rejoiced. "Carol will be thrilled," Jix exclaimed.

Pondering the wisdom of dropping in unannounced on Clifford Purefoy, Abby Gayle asked as they walked into the foyer, "Marigold, I suppose you are aware that Bryson's grandfather is experiencing dementia. He had to be excused from the last meeting we attended. It's common knowledge he isn't mentally stable."

Marigold stopped abruptly, threw her red-orange head back, and burst out laughing. "Mentally stable, my eye! The man is a drunk! An alcoholic! He hasn't been sober a day since Yolanda died and left him with that brat of a grandson. Ha! Dementia! That's hogwash!" She roared with laughter.

Abby Gayle's jaw dropped. Jix's eyes widened, and she momentarily stopped breathing.

"I've never heard anyone say the man drinks. Surely it would be obvious to those who know and work with him." Jix said. "Mother hasn't said he drinks."

"Honey, he holds his liquor well. Clifford is a closet drunk. He sneak-drinks. The man would rather die a slow death than admit he downs Vodka like a fish drinks water. Alcohol doesn't have a smell…booze-breath comes from booze that contains hops, barley, and other stuff. Vodka is his choice of drinks…no booze breath for Clifford.

"I suppose he may have pickled his brain by now." She

pondered the possibility. "It's more likely he's pickled his liver. Your mother knows he's a boozer but is too kind to say so. This type of alcoholism is the sort no one talks about. People talk more openly about venereal diseases. Addiction comes in many flavors, ladies. The world is full of closet alcoholics. They drive. They work. Many are prominent leaders. Some are at the church every time the door opens. Drunk as skunks. Playing a role. Living a lie. Come on. Let's catch Clifford before he gets soused…if he hasn't already."

Chapter Forty

The car window lowered as Jix glided to a stop. Marigold leaned forward and yelled past Jix at a speaker box on the gate post, "Harold, it's Marigold Fairmont. Open the gate! And you are out of a job if you tell Old Purefoy I'm here. Trust me on that," she threatened.

In the back seat, Abby Gayle dropped her head into her hands. She looked up at Jix's eyes reflected in the rearview mirror. Abby Gayle shrugged her shoulders; Jix grinned.

The wrought iron gate swung open. "Push the button again," Marigold said to Jix. Harold's monotone voice answered.

"Open the door to the sunroom, Harold. And make it snappy!" Marigold adjusted the sling on her shoulder, pulled down the sun visor, and flipped open the mirror. When satisfied she was presentable, she snapped it shut and directed Jix to a parking spot in the side yard of the sprawling ranch-style estate.

Met by the housekeeper, Marigold strutted into a sunshine-flooded room with Jix and Abby Gayle lagging behind.

"I'm concerned for Mr. Purefoy." Abby Gayle leaned close and whispered.

"He deserves what he gets. Surely, he knew he'd be taking on Marigold when he attempted to hijack Fairmont Foundation," Jix whispered in return.

"Where is the old fool, Mayetta?" She breezed past a housekeeper rendered speechless.

Marigold sashayed down the hallway, her high heels clicking like castanets on the polished hardwood floor. She burst into the library to confront an unsuspecting man who bore the symptoms of someone trapped in a brain fog.

Clifford Purefoy, sitting at his desk, sprang to his feet, spilling the last of a small glass of tomato juice he'd been sipping. A sense of dread knitted his eyebrows into one.

"What is happening? You can't barge in here this time of morning. I'll have you all thrown out!" He roared, frantically dabbing at the spill with a napkin.

"Sit down, you jackass!" Marigold pushed him with her unfettered hand. Caught off balance, he fell back into the chair.

"This is ridiculous!" He sputtered a crisp retort. "Unhand me, woman!"

Jix and Abby Gayle exchanged glances. *Unhand me?*

"Shut up and listen, you old fool!" She whisked a pile of papers onto the floor and parked her backside on the corner of the desk. "This is no more ridiculous than what you've allowed to happen to the Fairmont Foundation. I trusted you! But, no more! You've ridden the Fairmont train to the end of the line. For Yolanda's sake, the foundation and I have overlooked your inebriated behavior for years, but you've gone too far this time, Cliff. The jig is up!"

Jix and Abby Gayle sat across the desk quietly viewing the scene as if they were watching the nightly news.

"It's all over but the final bow, hot shot." She looked at his wrinkled hands shaking. "Did you spill your first Bloody Mary of the day?" she mocked. "Well, you're not getting another drop of alcohol until you tell us what this charade is all about.

Start with why! Why were you so anxious to get your hands on Fairmont Manor? At my expense, I might add. What was your incentive to toss me out on the street?"

The man with an ample crop of frosted hair dropped his head and calmly stated. "Sit down properly, Marigold. This is unbecoming to a woman of your stature."

He looked up at her. "Why don't I have Mayetta bring us coffee, and yes, I prefer mine with a bit of a boost. This is, of course," he nodded to the ladies seated across from him, "an acquired taste, and not for everyone."

Soothed by Abby Gayle's diplomatic insistence, Marigold pulled up a chair within arm's reach of the elderly Purefoy. He rang for coffee and then went across the room to the bar to get a decanter of liquor. Placing the crystal bottle on his desk, he sat down, folded his hands, and leaned back in the chair. He hadn't expected the freedom bestowed by openly admitting he drank.

"You are correct, my dear Marigold. No more secrets. It is time to right a wrong. I'm tired, and my regrets are more than a few." He rolled his eyes to the ceiling and sighed. "This all began with a slip of the tongue. My tongue, to be precise."

The maid entered with a tray of coffee and biscotti. She poured her employer a cup to which he added a 'boost'. He closed his eyes as he sipped.

Poof! The temporary truce vanished.

Marigold shouted, "Oh, come on, Clifford! Spare us the melodrama. Get on with it! Tell us what you know, or you can tell it from the witness stand."

Jix had to bite her cheek to stifle a chuckle. *Truly, they broke the mold when they made Marigold.*

"Dear woman," he addressed his infuriated, uninvited guest. "If you'll give me a moment, please. You asked for an explanation. May I talk… without being interrupted?"

Marigold answered with silence.

"I went to work for Joel Fairmont sixty years ago. If I

remember correctly, you were eighteen or nineteen at the time; I was not much older." He paused to pin down the exact year, "In nineteen and twenty-nine." He sipped his drink. To everyone's amazement, Marigold uttered not a word. Perhaps she was remembering the good years.

He met her gaze. "My dear, dear, Marigold, you've somehow come to believe you control everything within your world. May I have the distinct honor of informing you that nothing could be further from the truth? I have harbored a secret for most of your lifetime. I mistakenly told my wife, and on her deathbed, she swore me to a plan that I neither initiated nor endorsed."

With a steadier hand, he refilled his cup. After a long, uncomfortable silence, Clifford continued.

"Bryson was Yolanda's only grandchild, and she wanted him to have what is rightfully yours. I couldn't reason with her. My wife was dying a painful death, so, reluctantly, I promised her I'd reveal in a letter to Bryson a matter of great importance that no one but your father and I knew...that is until I foolishly told her. Yolanda insisted I tell Bryson and no one else. I'd intended for the letter to be opened when my estate was settled. Unfortunately, when Bryson retrieved a few things for me from my safety deposit box, he found it. I'd forgotten the letter was there. He opened it, and nothing has been the same since. If there is any pleasure to come from this debacle...this disastrous fiasco...it will come from the sheer delight I receive from seeing your face when you know what I wrote."

He pushed the chair back and stood. "It is time for this to come to a head. Let's take a ride, ladies. I'll give Bryson a call and tell him I want to talk to him. Perhaps I'll forget to mention three lovely damsels will accompany me."

Chapter Forty-One

Cupping her hand over the telephone receiver, Jix whispered, "Yes, can you meet us there? We are leaving now." She had lingered behind while Abby Gayle saw Marigold and Clifford to the car.

When plans with Detective Bird were in place, Jix drove her passengers to meet Bryson.

In the bright light of day, *I Digg It Supper and Social Club* looked like every other building on the block. The club's neon signs were as dormant as vampires until sundown.

Jix parked in the alley, and Clifford led the way to the employee's entrance. The four climbed the same staircase Jix and Abby Gayle had taken on their previous visit, pausing for Marigold to catch her breath and for her to warn Clifford he'd best not be up to devious tricks.

At the end of the corridor, Clifford walked into Clancy Diggs' office without knocking and then held the door until the women were inside, allowing fresh air into the unventilated room.

Diggs sat at his desk, a cigar smoldering in an ashtray. In the background, Cher toyed with the notion of turning back time.

Bryson sprawled over a leather chair with his legs crossed at the ankles, a drink in his hand. Taken aback, both men demanded an explanation as to what the elder Purefoy wanted and why the women were with him.

Tension in the room was as tight as a piano string. Marigold's contemptuous glare clearly conveyed an unspoken message to Diggs and Bryson that she need not check with them as to where she chose to be.

Clifford interrupted Bryson's harsh objections, "I've told Marigold and her friends about the letter you opened and how you've allowed greed to possess you. I haven't told them what I wrote in the letter, but I'm going to. It's over, Bryson. You and Diggs have created a diabolical mess. I'm ashamed of you...and of myself."

Steeped in hubristic pride, Bryson's chin jutted out; his nostrils dilated; his eyes flashed defiance. *Diabolical indeed!*

Diggs wrapped his fingers around the cigar and irately drew on it until the tip glowed bright red. Blowing smoke, he uttered to Bryson through clinched teeth, "I wish I'd never laid eyes on you, Purefoy. You are a disaster waiting to happen."

Marigold tuned up. "You're one to talk! Talk about the pot calling the kettle black! I...."

The desk phone bellowed incessantly. Diggs snatched the receiver, listened, and then said "Gottcha!" He launched forward and landed with a jolt.

"The cops are here again. Out! All of you! Get out of here!" Barking insults, he herded the visitors to the door and into the hallway. The door slammed; the lock clicked.

"Well! Of all the nerve! I've been thrown out of better places!" Her head snapped back, her chin tilted upward, her gaze zipped down her nose like a skier on a snowy slope. With a feline attitude of indifference, Marigold sniffed and haughtily adjusted her sling.

Clifford shook his head. "I'm so sorry, Marigold. This should have never happened."

"Redemption lies in repentance, Clifford. Fix this mess!"

Word the police were on the premises spread rapidly. Two women fled past on their way to the stairs. Jix recognized one as the girl in the red bustier and fishnet stockings. Over her shoulder, she tossed a tip their way. "Try the next door down. It opens into that room."

Jix grabbed Marigold's arm. "You and Mr. Purefoy go to the car. We'll be along shortly."

Marigold hesitated, prepared to object. Before she could protest, Abby Gayle urged her and Clifford to do as Jix said. "Go, Marigold. There's nothing more you can do here. You may see Detective Bird on your way out. Tell her where we are. Now hurry, but be careful going down the stairs."

"I'll help her," Clifford said.

Marigold informed him, in no uncertain terms, if help were available to the needy, he should step to the head of the line.

The room from which they'd been ousted was vacant. "They've escaped through the bookcase. We have to find how to open it." Jix dashed to where she'd seen the door close when they'd first witnessed Diggs' disappearance.

Both women were drawn to a bust of Shakespeare on a pedestal. They turned it this way and that. "If music be the food of love, play on," Abby Gayle quoted.

"Romeo and Juliet?" Jix queried.

"Twelfth Night."

The sculpture was nothing more than a bust of the poet, quill in hand.

Jix ran her fingertips across the tops of books and along the edge of the bookcase to no avail.

"This could be it." Abby Gayle reached toward a bronzed

bookend of *The Thinker*. Fingering the contemplative figure's head, she pulled it toward her.

Nothing happened.

Jix searched the shelf. "It's a bookend. Where's the other one?"

At the far end of a row of books, she located the matching theorist. Wrapping her fingers around the head of the figure, she pulled it forward. When nothing happened, she pushed it in the opposite direction.

To their sheer delight, the bookcase silently swung around, and without hesitation, they ducked behind it.

An ordinary corridor led to a spacious room lined with shelves and filled with tables. Televisions, computers, cameras, small and large appliances, household goods, electronic devices —some with price tags still attached—sat on every available surface.

"What is all this?" Jix moved around the room taking it all in. She spotted the steel door to a walk-in vault safe.

Abby Gayle speculated, "Stolen goods, maybe?" S h e lifted the lid off a plastic bin. "Look at this. How odd."

Jix took the hand-size bag she held out and examined it. "Rock salt?"

"That's what the label says. There must be hundreds of bags in here." She dug down. "This is different." She pulled out a bag the same size as the others. "The label is the same, but the texture is different."

"I wish Carol was here; she'd know if this is heroin or something else." Jix continued to uncover bags of the white powder.

Bryson Purefoy's unmistakable deep-pitched tone resounded, "That's exactly what it is."

Startled, Jix dropped the bag back into the bin. Bryson barged into the room. "Diggs!" he shouted.

Abby Gayle carefully replaced the lid. "Is there anything you won't do, Bryson?"

Before he could answer, angrily, Diggs stormed in. "This is all your fault, Purefoy! Now look what you've done!"

"What did I do? I had no idea the old man was bringing anybody!"

"We have to get rid of them. Just what I needed today!" Diggs sarcastically exclaimed, his dark eyes raging with contempt. "I'll call downstairs and see if the cops are gone. We'll take them to the quarry. Perfect timing; blasting is scheduled for in the morning. There won't be enough remains to make an identification."

Jix countered, "The police know we are here. I called them before we left the Purefoy estate. And if you care to remember, both Marigold and Bryson's grandfather know we are in the building."

Diggs threw up his hands and spit out a string of profanities. "Now what?"

Bryson took a coiled rope off a table. "They may know the women are here, but the cops don't know about the passage to these rooms. We have time to get away. I'll tie them up."

"Forget it, you idiot! Let's just get out of here!"

The villains had no way of knowing the police knew about the secret rooms, thanks to Jix and Abby Gayle who exchanged smug glances.

Agreeing they should not waste another minute, the men turned to leave.

With no thought of possible consequences, Jix instinctively grabbed Bryson by his coattail as he turned to leave. She dodged a swift pirouette, and in a split-second landed a full force hit with her knee to his testicles. The dimpled-cheek man doubled over in excruciating pain, which Jix humanely alleviated by rendering him unconscious with a nearby toaster oven.

Meanwhile, Abby Gayle discovered that Clancy Diggs was small but strong. She grabbed him by the collar. In a split-second, he spun around and butted her with his head, paralyzing her diaphragm so her lungs couldn't inflate.

She stumbled backwards, unable to catch a breath. He bolted for the door.

Abby Gayle grabbed a saucer off a stack of dinnerware on the nearest table. With a flick of her wrist, she sailed it like a Frisbee, striking Clancy's head. He slammed into the doorframe and collapsed on the floor.

The women held each other tightly, shaken and breathless. It had all happened quickly and unintentionally. "Bill must never know," Jix uttered the first thought that came to mind.

Catching her breath, Abby Gayle said, "I can't believe we just did that! What possessed us?"

"Desperation. We couldn't let them get away."

"Good job, Sherlock. Note that we should avoid hand-to-hand combat whenever possible."

"Let's check into taking a martial arts course." A high-five slap brought an "Ouch" from Abby Gayle.

Detectives Bird and Martino, accompanied by two officers, burst into the room, weapons drawn.

"Sorry, we had to start without you," Jix said.

Chapter Forty-Two

"Tell me again, so I don't miss a detail." Wearing boxer shorts and white socks, Bill snapped a retractable measuring tape in and out of its casing. He had measured the wall Jix planned to paper and written his findings, minus space occupied by three windows, on the back of an envelope. Thinking ahead, he'd measured both the solid wall and the window-wall because she hadn't settled on which one would be papered.

Barefooted, legs crossed, Jix sat on the carpet dressed in shorts and a tank top. "Flash back to the late twenties, early thirties," she said. "Joel Fairmont, known to be a savvy businessman, foresaw the stock market crash and the Great Depression looming on the horizon. He converted his assets into gold, and ingeniously, he had the gold applied to rolls of wallpaper with a technique that allows it to be removed. I think this was done in France."

Now was as good a time as any to propose a trip abroad. "I'd really like to take a trip to Versailles. Abby Gayle and I have talked about it." She lay on her back with her legs together and lifted them toward the ceiling. Ten leg lifts and she rolled to her side to do lifts from that position.

Bill sat on his side of the bed fiddling with something in the nightstand drawer. "How did Clifford Purefoy find out about the gold?"

"He worked for Joel Fairmont as an accountant." She rested while she talked. "I don't think he ever told how he found out, just that he had discovered what had taken place. He was sworn to secrecy, and being a loyal employee, he kept the secret. Papa Fairmont may have paid him to keep quiet or compensated him handsomely in some way. Mr. Purefoy didn't say that had taken place. I'm just supposing."

Clifford reflected on the years that had passed while Joel Fairmont's fortune hung on the walls. His employer and friend died before stating his wishes as to what was to be done with the gold. Clifford wanted to tell Marigold, but he'd kept the secret from her for so long, he couldn't bring himself to share it. He planned to leave her a letter revealing the truth.

"So, let me get this straight." Bill moved to her side of the bed, sat down, and crossed his arms. "Just before she died, Purefoy, grieving and possibly under the influence of alcohol, unintentionally told his wife about the gold. He promised to tell Bryson and not Marigold. His wife believed the boy would find a way to obtain ownership of the property and take possession without Marigold ever knowing."

His wife completed the tenth push-up, stood, bounced energetically to the chaise lounge, and made herself comfortable. "A promise made is a promise kept, but Clifford didn't say he would tell Bryson immediately. His plan was for Bryson to find out when he read the letter—which he did, just before, not after, the grandfather's death...as planned."

Bill came over to the chaise and slid Jix's legs over so he could sit down.

"Greed gnaws like a cancer. I suppose Bryson told Clancy about the gold, and they hatched a plan to commandeer the property, so they could rob it." He patted her leg and leaned over to kiss her.

Heading for the bathroom to put on his pajamas, he asked, "From what you've told me, it appears Bryson got in a hurry and insisted his lawyer send the notice to Eva before he had fully executed the dissolution of the foundation. He may have promised the lawyer a hefty bonus."

"Bill, he lies when the truth would do. Bryson is very immature. Marigold pegged him as spoiled, but just between us, that's not his only shortcoming. I'm fairly certain he was not valedictorian of his class if you catch my drift."

He laughed. "I checked, and the current price of gold is $411.60 an ounce. What happens next?" Bill had stretched out in bed.

"All that is attached to the walls, which undoubtedly amounts to a sizable chunk, belongs to the Fairmont Foundation. That could well be as Joel Fairmont intended. Marigold has twelve rolls; those belong to her. I can keep the six rolls she gave me. Waldo is making arrangements for the paper to be removed and the gold converted into dollars. Marigold is not happy about the paper coming down. Even so, she knows leaving it is not a safe option should word get out 'there's gold in them thar hills'…or walls in this case."

"What are we talking…two ounces per roll…three, four?"

"You're more reliable at estimating how much. I haven't a clue; they look to be double-sized rolls. What do you think about us planning a trip to France next summer, or better yet, let's go in the spring…April or May? With the money from the paper, we can treat the Kamps to airfare and lodging… and Mother if she wants to go. We'll make it the vacation of a lifetime."

"Count me in."

Jix pondered a random thought. Her sister, Reggie, an upcoming fashion designer, had been to France. She even spoke the language; although Jix wasn't sure how fluently.

"You know what? Reggie is getting married. She may want to go with us to shop for a wedding dress."

"Keep in mind total expenses if you are thinking of treating her to airfare and accommodations. Wait until you find out how much the gold will bring. Let's don't get carried away and end up in debt."

"I know. I'd like to take the Watson boys, and Eva, and the Shepherd sisters, and Sonya, and...."

A light tap on the door, and in ran Dinah smelling of scented bubble bath and dressed for bed in pink polka-dotted pajamas and tiny bunny slippers. Caught up in the excitement, Willowdean barked her *happy bark*.

Carol asked if they were intruding.

"Certainly not," Jix sat up and patted the chaise for Carol to sit beside her. Dinah scrambled across the bed and dove into her granddad's outstretched arms. Willowdean jumped on the bed then off when Carol called her. Bill got up to sit on the floor and play with his granddaughter.

Jix and Carol talked about Lisandra and predicted a favorable outcome with proper treatment and support, albeit she would eventually be held accountable for assault and kidnapping. They agreed that Bryson's dirty deeds of forgery and fraud were not his greatest offenses. Drug dealing would put him away for years. Clancy was charged with a gamut of crimes ranging from possession of drugs, smuggling drugs, fencing stolen property... to name a few.

"Marigold is setting up college funds for the Watson kids. She has arranged for the Watsons to live at Fairmont Manor rent-free for as long as they choose to stay. That will permit Belinda to work one job and give her more time with her family. And through the foundation, the Shepherd sisters will be provided for...possibly for the rest of their lives."

"What about Ryan?" Carol asked.

"He'll live where Aaron lived. He does odd jobs for Marigold, and he helps Eva with maintenance. The units on the two vacant floors will be repaired, remodeled, and rented. All tenants who want new appliances or renovation to their apartments only need to ask. The old building will get the facelift it needs and deserves. The Fairmont Foundation's coffers are overflowing."

"Will they close the tunnel?"

"Not if the Watson boys have anything to say about it," Carol laughed. She reached in her pocket. "Here. This is what I came to show you. I found this in the junk drawer in the kitchen when I was looking for the lid to my thermos."

Unfurling the tiny strip of paper from the fortune cookie she'd tossed in the drawer and forgotten, Jix read aloud, "An inch of time is an inch of gold."

"That's spooky," Carol said.

"That is coincidental," Bill underscored. He helped Dinah slide her slippered feet into Jix's shoes she'd left by the bed.

"Yoohoo!" Margee called from the staircase. "Look who I found on our doorstep."

"Visitors?" Jix looked at the clock on the bureau. Ten till nine.

Austin Kamp's boyish good looks filled the doorway. "Hope we've not come calling too late. If we have, just tell us to go home."

Bill stood to shake Austin's hand. "We've been to eat, and on the way home, we saw your lights on and thought we'd stop in for a minute. Actually, we're leaving in the morning for three days in Florida and wanted to see you before we go."

"Glad you came by. Sit down, or we can go downstairs where we can be more comfortable." Bill offered to make coffee.

Margee and Abby Gayle, happily entertained by a two- year-old, steadied Dinah as she wobbled in her grandmother's shoes.

Abby Gayle declined coffee, saying they could only stay a short time. She sat down on the end of the bed. Carol moved over for Margee to sit on the chaise with her and Jix. Bill pulled out the stool to Jix's dresser for Austin. Right away, the conversation turned to Clancy Diggs.

"Why did he turn Lisandra against the Shepherd sisters and Marigold? If he did, in fact, have such a strategy," Austin asked.

Jix pointed out that Stacy Shepherd could tie Clancy to Bryson because of the research she'd done. He wanted her out of the way.

Margee spoke up. "I think his ultimate goal was to take Marigold out of the picture. She was their main obstacle in securing the property, so they could steal a fortune. If Lisandra killed the sisters in a jealous rage, then turned on Marigold, Clancy and Bryson would be free to get the tenants out of the building. By the way, the Foundation is being completely restructured. Charles Pennington is going to chair the Board. I trust nothing like this business with Bryson will ever happen again."

"What will happen to Clifford Purefoy?" Carol asked.

"A good lawyer can get him off," Austin said. "He has dementia, you know."

Bill said in a burst of enthusiasm, "Let's move on to cheerier things. My wife is going to take us to Paris with her windfall." He clapped his hands. "Who wants to go?"

Dinah, sitting in Abby Gayle's lap clapped her hands. "Go," she said and waved bye-bye.

"I'd love to, but I can't miss work." Carol stood to leave. "We're saving to buy a house when Scotty gets back."

Margee didn't want to go anywhere and said her passport had expired since she'd honeymooned in Paris. She and Carol would hold down the fort while the others traveled.

Carol noted it was past Dinah's bedtime and gathered her sleepy toddler in her arms. Austin and Abby Gayle left when Carol did, and Margee soon followed.

Alone again, Jix crawled into bed. "Let's talk about our trip."

She turned off the light, pulled the cover under her chin, and smiled in the dark. Friends and family had filled her heart with love and laughter.

"I'm ready to look at the inside of my eyelids," Bill chuckled. "This has been a day of tireless chatter. Let's just listen to the silence, sweetheart."

She backed up to him in their familiar spoon position.

He snuggled her close.

"*Bonne nuit, Chérie.*" He kissed her ear. "I'm so glad you stayed out of the way and let Detective Bird do her job."

When she didn't comment, he asked, "You *did* stay out of the way and let her do her job, didn't you?"

"I helped when I could, but, of course, Detective Bird is always in charge," she said.

THE END

Made in USA - Kendallville, IN
1098330_9780999478554
05.04.2020 1640